Weir

of the

Great Lakes

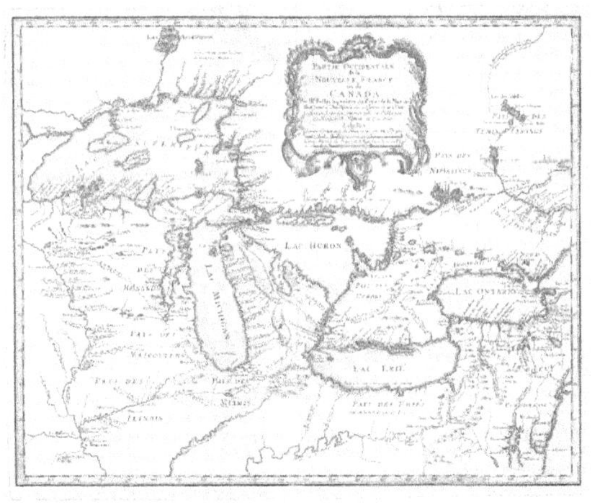

by

Aleco Julius

ISBN: 9798218416966

Publication History

"Glacial Eternal" originally appeared in *Dark Matter Magazine* Issue 017

"The Seven Mysterious Drownings of the SS *Neptune*" originally appeared in *Anterior Skies* Vol. I (Strange Elf Press)

Weird Tales
of the
Great Lakes

For my everyday supporters,

Alex, Vivi, & Becca

"... through a vast unknown of barbarism, poured its turbid floods into the bosom of its gentle sister."

–Father Jacques Marquette

There are souls beneath that water.
Fixed in Slime they speak their piece.

–Dante Alighieri

"They are swept by Borean and dismasting blasts as direful as any that lash the salted wave; they know what shipwrecks are, for out of sight of land, however inland, they have drowned full many a midnight ship with all its shrieking crew."

–Herman Melville

"A normal lake is knowable. A Great Lake can hold all the mysteries of an ocean, and then some."

–Dan Egan

No unhallowed breath shall seal a fate before me,
Join the drowned in the silence of the black lake's womb.

–Agalloch

—Father Jacques Marquette

Table of Contents

Glacial, Eternal

It all began with a mysterious find. In the summer of 2019, a small team of underwater archeologists from the University of Chicago was traversing the waters of Lake Michigan, in search of both a lost shipwreck and cultural artifacts. Specifically, they were looking for the SS *Neptune*- which had foundered during a storm in the 1840s- and gathering samples of the lakebed for multidisciplinary study. Half of the six-person team was made up of graduate students, led by Department of Archaeology Professor, Mills Knox.

They were working in partnership with the *Midwest Prehistory Society,* and so anthropologist Dr. Cassandra Luna was invited on board. She had recently published her book *The World of Cahokia,* about the great prehistoric city of the Mississippian people, and thus her knowledge of the region and its history was invaluable. Things had gone smoothly over the first few days, though the ominous third day of the project proved difficult to explain.

Professor Knox's previous success in locating wrecks of both seafaring vessels and aircraft earned his team the funding to acquire state-of-the-art sonar equipment and remote submarine vehicles. He had published his most recent find in *The Journal of Inland Seas,* in which he detailed his location of the two-masted schooner *Dusk,* which sank in Lake Huron during the Great Gale of 1913. In fact, the August 4, 2019 edition of the *Muskegon Register* ran a short article about the new shipwreck project. Dr. Luna was interviewed, in which she said, "This is an exciting opportunity. It's always a privilege to be able to explore the lakebed, where clues are sometimes found of the past cultures and peoples who lived there before the lakes as we know them."

On the morning of Wednesday, August 6, Professor Knox and Dr. Luna launched their sixty-foot dive boat from the 59th Street docks near campus. With them were the pilot, Lenny Johns, who was also an experienced Lake Michigan boater, and three graduate students: Kiara Bellfield, April Albati, and Lazaro Toribio. The day was productive, with several vials of lakebed samples recovered from forty feet below. The three graduate students made good use of the rigorous diving program they had completed earlier that summer. There was no sign, however, of the steamship for which they had been searching.

The second day it stormed. In the late morning, the distant thunder rumbled lazily across the water from the west. The surface was altered from tranquil azure to turbulent gray. No luck with wreckage, but they had an hour's diving time before the tempest arrived. Hurrying back to land, the team was excited to go into the lab for inspection of the first two days' collections. They had unearthed the broken shells of zebra mussels, fish bones, and rocks of various types among the silt. Half a year later, Bellfield told the *Chicago Reader,* "It was pretty standard stuff, at first. But then Laz found the one that changed everything."

After a few hours of examining samples, Bellfield and Albati decided to go for a late lunch at a nearby noodle shop. They stood up from their microscope stations and crossed the room toward Toribio. Luna was entering data on her computer while Knox packed up some papers for a meeting on another floor of the building. No one had yet noticed the strange body language of Lazaro Toribio. As the women approached him, he was as still as a transfixed statue, holding a stone about the size of a large fist in his hands. Albati recalled, "I guess that was the first sign, but at the time we didn't think anything of it. We had to call his name out a few times to get his attention, so we thought he was tired, or maybe hungry or something." Bellfield concurred: "He looked tired or sick. You know, come to think of it, after all that happened the next day... he looked a little scared."

At that point, Professor Knox took his leave for the meeting and told them all he would head home afterward and see them at the docks early the next day. Dr. Luna turned her attention to the grad students. On episode twelve of the *Curious Phenomena* podcast, recorded in 2021, she described her meeting with what we now call the Heart Stone: "It sounds silly for me to say this about a rock, but there's no other way to explain it. It was like a negotiation, a source that was new to me. Not just to me as an individual, but to something. Something deeper." She goes on to elaborate how she felt her breath quicken and her hands tremble. "Was it nausea?" She shrugged. "It was probably just the heat of the lab and the humidity outside." The average daytime temperature of the first two days was eighty-eight degrees Fahrenheit, ninety-three with the heat index.

Toribio snapped out of his stupor, waving off any concerns that he was not okay. The three grad students called it a day and walked to their eating spot. But Dr. Luna stayed behind, enraptured by the odd stone. At a glance, she noticed discolored markings on the dull, silver-colored specimen. Taking a closer look, they appeared to be petroglyphs of some kind, but they were nothing like anything she had come across in her extensive research. The overlapping ellipses seemed too patternlike to have occurred randomly. On the podcast, she states, "To my knowledge, they were unknown, especially amid the region of the Great Lakes. I decided to take a fresh look in the morning. But that feeling of vertigo didn't totally go away."

When the crew convened at eight o'clock the next morning by the docks, the heat was already stifling. The students held their duffel bags of equipment in one hand, cold brew coffees in the other. Lenny Johns, the pilot, was preparing the boat for launch, checking off in his head all the safety and readiness measures he had performed a thousand times before. Albati and Bellfield remembered the moments before embarkation on their third day of exploration. Albati recalled, "We planned on getting out on the lake early to beat the heat, but it was already hot as hell. Laz was quieter than normal, but he insisted to me and Kiara that he was fine."

Off to the side, Dr. Luna was explaining the bizarre stone to Professor Knox, who was intently nodding along as she spoke. Knox was initially incredulous, but trusted the expertise of Luna, and they both agreed to examine it together that afternoon. As for Johns, he noticed that something was different. On the *Discovery* YouTube channel documentary segment about the Heart Stone event and its subsequent consequences, he affirmed, "It just didn't feel right, but I suppose it was the heat and humidity messing with my head. I suggested that they postpone until another day, but they wouldn't hear of it. We had plenty of drinking water on board, and the lake was pretty calm, so I can't blame them for what happened."

The first dive of the day was to be made by Dr. Luna, Bellfield, and Toribio. Johns cut the engine of the boat about five hundred yards out, where the steamship supposedly went down. Sonar work detected nothing but low ridges and commonplace sandbars beneath the waves. Dr. Luna was more eager to detects signs of prehistoric human life than sunken wrecks, and looked forward to gathering ample material for study. So, they donned their scuba gear and splashed into the water with tools in hand. After twenty-five minutes, Dr. Luna gave the signal to ascend. It wasn't until they climbed back aboard the dive boat, however, that they realized Toribio wasn't with them. It was immediately concerning, as the dangers of lake diving can strike during the most routine of situations.

"Well, of course. Before I took my gear off, I went right back in," recalled Dr. Luna. "I had plenty more oxygen in the tank, and plus, Laz's behavior from the previous day cropped up in my mind. Maybe he'd passed out or something." But there was no sign of Lazaro Toribio. It was at that moment, within the tenebrous depths of the lake, that she felt the indistinct grip of the Heart Stone and vaguely recognized its dread import.

She resurfaced minutes later. Lenny Johns started up the boat, ready to circle the area. In the ensuing days, a report by the *Consortium for Lake Michigan Water Safety* concluded that there should have been no rip currents in the area of their sampling, which was the original conviction of both Johns and Knox. As the boat began to move, there was an abrupt breach in the surface, accompanied by a loud gasp. Toribio had appeared to the relief of all, looking quite pale. Although a good swimmer, he struggled to stay afloat. Bellfield described the scene: "Laz was shaking, not swimming. Like, violently shaking. When they pulled him up out of the water, I could see the crystals on his mask."

Knox took Toribio in his arms. "He was in shock, and I was in shock. I couldn't believe it. He was ice cold and shivering like a hypothermic despite the relatively warm water and the excessive heat that day. It didn't make any sense." In the *Discovery* video, Johns spoke from his boat out on the lake. "We were right about here. When that kid came out of the water, it may just as well have been the damn Arctic Circle."

As his fellow grad students wrapped him up with towels, Dr. Luna sensed a shift in the atmosphere, a prickling sensation like that of an impending storm, or the awesome, terrifying indifference of the open sea. Johns swung the boat toward shore and shifted into high gear. Dr. Luna was phoning paramedics to meet them at the docks when Toribio spoke. "Why- Why did you leave me down there for so long?" After a collective hesitation, Professor Knox said, "We're sorry, Laz. But did you get turned around down there? How did you end up getting lost?" To which Toribio replied, "You left me there all night." His teeth continued to chatter, but his breathing stabilized a bit and a touch of color returned to his face.

Back on land, there was a perceptible dissolution of the young man that had been Lazaro Toribio. He did not respond to questions and was reticent toward the rest of the team. He allowed the paramedics, who had been waiting at the docks, to examine him. They did in fact diagnose him with hypothermia, which brought on a volley of unanswerable questions. One of the emergency medical technicians, Ava Thomas, wrote the following in Mitchell

Hospital's official report, dated August 8, 2019: "Expected to treat for water ingestion and near drowning. Symptoms of Hypothermia? Shivering, disorientation, memory loss. Skin on face and extremities exhibit possible frostbite. Refused ambulance."

Toribio abruptly left toward his dorm room, about a 15-minute walk. The team desperately attempted to reason with him, but to no avail. His drowsy stupor was similar to the previous day's, Dr. Luna thought. "And what did he mean that we left him in the lake overnight? If he blacked out, how did he survive?" These words are from the *Chicago Reader* story published in the spring of 2020, called "The Heart Stone Enigma." Later that afternoon, Bellfield and Albati stopped by Toribio's dorm room. They knocked and called his phone, but there was no response. The boundless force at lake's bottom had already taken its hold.

Dr. Luna spent the evening of the third fateful day examining the Heart Stone with Professor Knox. Both were unnerved and somewhat vertiginous with bafflement. According to Dr. Luna, it could not be categorized as an artifact of indigenous peoples. Careful scrutiny of the elliptical markings revealed faded dotting and an embedded, veined network design. Knox felt as though he were "holding a piece of fruit, or an egg, not a stone. There were characteristics of organic material, but at the same time, it reacted to tests as though it were a mineral." After the incident, the exploration project was canceled, and the mysterious stone was stored in the lab.

While both scientists were well-seasoned in the realm of rocks, they called upon geologist Antony Eliad. In an article published in the Fall 2021 issue of *North American Geology*, he is quoted as saying, "Never seen anything like it. My first instinct was that it was chondrite. I've examined many meteorites in my career, but my studies of this particular stone were inconclusive. It was fascinating. Exhilarating, even. Like it had an invisible pulse." Additional testing by the group determined that the stone was billions of years old, far older than typical Great Lakes rocks, whose average years of age are merely in the hundreds of millions.

Lazaro Toribio did not take classes that fall. He became distant to his family and ignored friends and mentors at the university. Knox told the *Reader,* "It's a shame, because he was a brilliant student and a good guy besides. I made my efforts to reach him, like we all did, but no." Because he still paid tuition, room and board, and was a student in good standing, he was allowed to stay in his small 59th Street dorm apartment. "He did go to the libraries, though," said Bellfield. "I didn't see it myself, but that was the rumor. All through the fall, he was like a ghost making his way around campus. Very early in some of the cafeterias, and very late at the mini-marts, where he bought up hordes of food."

His library account records were made available to internal investigators, who in the end made no headway in determining an explanation for what happened in January 2020, soon after the Heart Stone went missing. Among the books Toribio checked out were Edmond Miller's *The Glacial Great Lakes,* Liana M. Cortina's *Cognition Rethought,* and Jaxson Oquendo's *The Phenomenology of Anatomy.* Assuredly, he was searching for meaning in his profound experience. Records show that he also purchased occult books online. Two of the volumes he bought from Watkins Books in London were Fr. Silvester Panizante's sixteenth-century treatise *Daemonologia Frigus,* and *The Grimoire of Sea and Sand* by Laurentia Beaumont.

Toribio was the chief suspect when the Heart Stone disappeared from the archeology laboratory just after the new year. As it turned out, of course, the suspicions proved correct. "Someone was pounding on my door," remembers Bellfield. "So, I open it, and he's standing there with his backpack. I FaceTimed April right away." Toribio appeared especially gaunt. His clothing was rumpled, and he had dark circles under his eyes.

Because it was Saturday night, January 4, Albati was staying at her parents' house in the western suburbs. Their class meetings had not yet resumed for the new year, meaning hardly anyone was around. This provided Toribio advantageous conditions to steal the stone. Since he still had his lab keys, there were no obstacles.

Bellfield had the wherewithal to use a recording app while the three grad students were on the video call, conversing together for the first time since the day Toribio had emerged from the water, sick with hypothermic chill. The recording was eventually obtained by university security.

What follows is an overview of that call.

Toribio: I've been unwell.

Albati: We just want to help you, Laz. Talk to us.

Toribio: I know I haven't been myself.

There is a pause.

Toribio: When I was down there, underwater, I encountered a being. It was a thing, a monstrous thing, an entity I believe, something incredibly old, with incredible knowledge. I didn't know this when it happened, but it's something I've thought a lot about.

Haven't thought about anything else at all, actually. You know how it is down there. The enveloping semi-darkness and the dappled light. Frightening, but at the same time sort of-- Sort of spiritual.

Both Albati and Bellfield's facial expressions conveyed a mixture of worry and fear.

Bellfield: What do you mean? We're worried about you.

Albati: What did it look like?

Toribio: It-- It was the color of opaque ice, and it emerged from the rippling shadows at the bottom of the lake. There were markings slashed all around it, with impurities here and there that resembled frozen deposits of mud and sand. And it was huge. Maybe about the size of a truck. Just a massive chunk of glacier. When it came for me, the water turned so cold. I could feel its presence, and through my mask, the weak light from the surface showed me its jagged shape."

Albati and Bellfield are silent for a moment, so Toribio goes on.

Toribio: It spoke to me. I heard its voice in my head. Not sure how to describe it, because there weren't any words, just ideas and concepts and images. I know what it wants.

Bellfield: Look, Laz, I'm so glad you came to me- to us- but we should go to someone who can--

Toribio cut her off: It wants this.

He slings his backpack around to his chest, zips it open, and extracts the Heart Stone. The women gasp.

Toribio: And I must take it back. Every day, at least once a day, I see in my mind's eye the dim, silent nadir of the lake. Staggering images of eldritch vistas, when glaciers ruled the continents for eons. I could feel the tension of our desires, our feeble grasping at knowledges lost to the depths of time, and the wild indifference of the ice.

Bellfield: Who are you right now?

Toribio: This agency, see, has always existed within the vast mountainous floes. Vital energies of terrestrial transformation. Before humans, and before the seas themselves. What I hold here in my hands is the ancient heart of the lakes.

Albati: But how did this all happen in a just a few minutes?

Toribio: To me it felt like day, a single revolution. The ice revealed to me how time moves for all matter and consciousness. Immeasurable gulfs for us are but fleeting moments for the agency within the ice.

Bellfield: This thing, this monster, tried to kill you. Don't you see that?

Toribio: No. It was the irresistible violence of extreme form. And so, my individuality was annihilated. With the gradual warmth of the lake, the heart stone was unlocked from the ice, where it had been positioned for immense durations, and released into the waters. Now it knows.

Albati: Knows what, Laz?

Toribio: Our time is up.

There is a flash of understanding in the faces of the women, the subtlest hint of the unthinkable.

The video ends as Toribio walks out without another word. Bellfield later reported that she "Tried to stop him, but it was completely pointless. It was like he was possessed." The only others she could trust to know the situation were Dr. Luna and Professor Knox, but by the time she reached them, Toribio must have been at the shoreline, frigid waves lapping at his feet on the gravelly sand in the darkness.

As soon as the students informed Dr. Luna of their call with Toribio, she intuited his mission. He would return to the frozen depths, to heed the beckoning call of cruel indifference. The entity would await his return in its obscure, cold lair, itself a solid anatomical mass of beguiling architecture.

That fall, Dr. Luna dug deep into the archeological and geological literature, researching the symbols on the Heart Stone and looking for clues of similar cases, but only found oblique references and unreliable anecdotes. She came across old myths and folklore that told of demons and magical creatures living among the icy crags near the poles. Antiquarian manuscripts that extolled the demiurgic soul of the iceberg. The book *From Stone to Star* by Claude Allegre offered intimations that the petroglyphs were a mode of writing, perhaps instructions of some kind. She also consulted renown cryptographer Olga Richtor, who suggested that the stone was a map. To Dr. Luna, that result was incomprehensible.

By the end of winter 2020, a report was completed by the Great Lakes Region Team at the *National Weather Service.* Compiling all the evidence, they concluded that an “ice water anomaly” was responsible for Toribio’s hypothermia, and that the brain damage he must have sustained from it contributed to his delusions.

Lazaro Toribio was not seen again. A recovery mission by the *Chicago Metropolitan Water Rescue* lasted three days, but amounted to nothing. Professor Knox lobbied to award a posthumous PhD in Archaeology to Toribio, which was received by his grieving family.

Eventually, Dr. Luna put some pieces of the puzzle together. She published her own article, "Student of the Waters," in the Winter 2022 issue of the magazine *Esoteric Sciences.*

This is an excerpt of her piece:

The voice of the ice was the voice of our foregone doom. And the paradox of our ephemeral lives, when weighed against the continental forces, is an apprehension both crushing and sublime. Through this submerged entity, this supposed anomaly, Lazaro glimpsed these magnitudes. He carried the burden of a knowledge that, in the end, was apparently too great to bear. He ached to return the Heart Stone to the murky depths, though it is my guess that his final act was in vain.

I imagine him stepping off the rocky beach and into the coaxing, black waves with an exalted feeling in his gut. Relieved to engage the glacial deity. Knowing that he would forever be a part of the eternal lake.

Extinct

"I haven't gone fishing in years," said Ervin. "I should buy a twelve pack and call up my boys. We could be at the lake in an hour."

"Shows you don't know shit about fishing," replied Fatima. "All the fish are out early in the morning. Before it's light, even. It's too late in the day to go fishing now."

Ervin admired the soft sheen on the russet-tinted reel of his new fishing rod. It was not quite new, exactly. But it was new to him, and appeared to be in pretty decent shape. The rod reminded him of the day his grandfather took him fishing at the cemetery pond as a kid. It was an idyllic scene that he associated with the carefree chapter of his childhood. Now his life was chock full of work, appointments, and headaches. Going fishing with his buddies would be a rare, well-earned break.

"Okay, tomorrow, then," said Ervin. "I got the day off. I'd like to try this baby out." His wife, Fatima, shrugged and went into the house.

Ervin held the rod in one hand and grabbed the rusty, green tacklebox with the other. The woman at the garage sale had thrown the tacklebox into the deal for a few extra bucks. Fifteen bucks total. It was the type of impulse buy reserved for flea market customers only, who take clandestine pleasure in browsing the miscellaneous detritus of a stranger's private life.

Without warning, the sounds of traffic, summer cicadas, and other random neighborhood noises abruptly died. His garage door was wide open, and he was thunderstruck by what he saw through it. Instead of his neighbors' houses and parked cars, he gaped with awe at sputtering volcanoes that towered to the dusky sky. In the place of well-trimmed lawns was a wild panoply of verdure, with vines crisscrossing between majestic treetops and in between great, gnarled trunks. In the distance he saw a green sea caked with foam past a rocky shore.

The hairs on the back of his neck stood up. Knees weak, he took a step toward the impossible outdoor scene. He opened his mouth and exhaled incomprehensibly.

"Garbage is full!" shouted Fatima from inside the house.

When he blinked, the bewildering scene was gone. Everything went back to normal. He could have sworn that at the last instant he had glimpsed an enormous insect buzzing past, like an effervescent dragonfly on steroids.

With shaking hands, he placed the fishing equipment in the trunk of his car. He searched his mind for some kind of explanation for this bizarre vision. *Maybe it was something I ate,* he thought. *Perhaps it was some kind of daydream,* he tried to reason. *Or maybe it was the knock to the head I took playing flag football last week. Yes, I'm sure it must have been that.*

He headed inside to throw out the trash. After that, he would call his buddies Ryland and Alejandro. Tell them to get their coolers ready for fishing tomorrow on Port Bay. He did not think either them had ever been fishing, but no matter. They would float carefree all day, and have a few beers while they were at it. *We work hard at the construction site, sometimes six or seven days a week,* thought Ervin. *We've earned it.*

The skies were overcast, but they decided to chance it and go fishing anyway. Ervin had rented a boat and extra rods online the previous evening, and the three friends drove to Lake Ontario's Port Bay before dawn. There were already several boats on the water when they left the dock, which was moments before the blaze of the sun painted the lake a golden hue. They carried their day's equipment between the three of them, including the tack-lebox full of the worms they picked up at a nearby gas station. The cooler held cans of beer on ice and ham sandwiches.

Scanning the rippling water in the morning light, Ervin's thoughts meandered back to the disquieting dream he had had a little while ago. In it, he had woken up to go fishing, but found himself all alone in the house. In fact, there was no one anywhere. No neighbors, and no other vehicles on the road when he got into his car and drove to the lake, which was also desolate and still as glass. He waded into the water from a pebbly beach and fell asleep at the bottom of the bay. It was good to be there, like a fetus enveloped by a warm elixir of nourishment. It felt right, to be rocked gently in the blue-blackness.

Then he woke up, and in waking life, took a quick shower before picking up Ryland and Alejandro. Fatima was still fast asleep. He kissed her lightly on the forehead before leaving. The dream had mostly faded as he hit the pre-dawn road, but he could not shake the sensation that a natural force was guiding him into uncharted waters.

Alejandro held a slippery earthworm between his fingers and planted it onto a hook. He handed one to Ervin, who held the wriggling specimen up to his face.

"This thing's got no idea what's about to happen to it," said Ervin. "I mean, think about it. Completely fucking oblivious. And here I am, like a god, about to put an end to its little, meaningless life."

"The hell you talking about, man?" Ryland stuck his hand in the crunchy ice of the cooler, pulled out a frosty can, and popped the top.

Gripping the handle of his fishing rod, Ervin flung it backward and then cast it forward. The reel unspooled with a satisfying sigh as the line arced over the waves. The dawn light had, for a split second, illuminated the line as it fell, like an un-helixed strand in the ether. The tiny, round bobber plopped onto the face of the lake. Ryland followed suit.

The size and shape of Port Bay lent itself to inlets of calm that still featured some decent catch. Of course,

Ervin and his friends had no real idea where the fish were, but that was not something they particularly minded.

To their surprise, after only minutes, there was a firm tug on Ervin's line. He hopped off the cooler and held the rod steady. Sure enough, the line became taut. With anticipation, the three friends gathered around. They noticed that, instead of attempting to break free, whatever hooked creature that was down there was swimming *toward* the boat. The line steadily cut through the water with a palpable sense of deliberation.

"Reel that fucker in," Alejandro hissed.

While Ervin turned the handle, goosebumps prickled his arms. The reeling-in was far too smooth. Though he hadn't gone fishing in years, his body remembered the tension created by a fish struggling to break free. That tension was absent now. Here again was the feeling that some force of nature was making its presence felt all around him—the sublime bay, the surrounding woods, the swirling insects. His friends were eager to see the catch, while, from the unknown depths, an irrational terror rose up and gripped Ervin by the throat.

When the thing breached the surface, a retching sound escaped Alejandro's lips. Ervin hoisted the rod high with an organism sagging at the end. Its amorphous blob of a head sprouted ten dangling arms. They all wiggled in obscene pleasure. Two rounded flaps emerged from each side of its head, which itself was the bulk of its gelatinous body. Black, beady eye holes bore their dumb stare into Ervin. The hook was buried in a protuberant siphon on its underside. The entire lump of moist, spotted fly was shaded a sickly jaundice.

Ervin, transfixed by the abomination, said, "Take it off the hook, Ry."

"I ain't touching that thing," Ryland said.

Alejandro crushed his empty beer can with one hand. "Good God," he said. "What is it?"

As if in response, the malformed thing slipped off the hook and fell at their feet with a wet smack. It quivered there at the bottom of the boat before the siphon started to gasp for air. The appendage elongated in strained desperation, sucking like mad. When, finally, it seemed as though it would wheeze its last syllable, the organism shot out its arms and gripped Ervin's ankles in a sticky, tentacular embrace. It climbed up his body like some grotesque, nautical spider, and wrapped around his midsection.

Instantly, a ferocious rush exploded into Ervin's consciousness, a flood of stimuli that obliterated his awareness of the here-and-now. He was pulled irresistibly through a radiant galaxy of light. He saw snowcapped mountains crumble to dust and rise again. He saw the totality of dense forestry collapse and grow anew. He witnessed oceans bubble in their infancy, and jungles invade the cracking continents and then retreat. Glaciers that carved out the contours of the world. Troglodytes and trilobites, the vast immeasurability of endless forms, to the timeless gulfs of nothingness, and the wonderful, unbridled terror that comes with it.

And in that space, where space is bereft of meaning, the point of potentiality that was called Ervin glimpsed the unfathomable. Contact with the origin. The ancestral.

The little fishing boat wobbled with the aftermath of commotion. Ryland and Alejandro had grappled with the squishy beast to no avail. It would not allow itself to be ripped off their friend. Instead, it lowered itself of its own accord, and splashed back into the lake without fanfare.

"You good, bro?" Alejandro asked. "I think you passed out."

"What happened? Where is it?" Ervin's head swiveled manically from side to side.

Ryland knelt by Ervin's side and helped him to sit up. As he did, he noticed crimson marks of indentation on Ervin's skin, where the creature's arms had clutched.

"What are we doing here? How long was I out?" asked Ervin, whose faced betrayed a bilious aspect. It was true that the sun was now fully above the horizon, but Ervin's confusion surpassed his reason.

"Hours?" Ryland said. "Man, it was only like a minute. Not even."

Ervin appeared as though he might black out again.

"Let's get the fuck outta here," said Alejandro.

Ryland started the motor to head back to shore, with Alejandro steering. The two friends shared an uncomfortable glance as, on the entire trip back, Ervin gazed over the side rail into the dark green waters. It was as if he had lost something down there, and was searching in hopeless despair for a suggestion of its return.

Fatima undressed for bed as her husband sat in the chair in the corner of their bedroom. She had closely observed him since he had returned early from his outing, and she was worried that his malaise was a symptom of some type of illness.

"You should take a shower, Ervin. The stink of that fish is still on you," Fatima said.

"It wasn't a fish," he replied. He raised himself with difficulty and stumbled to the bed. His whole body was stiff, a condition that had worsened throughout the day. Ryland and Alejandro had needed to help him out of the car and into the house. Ryland had also taken the wheel, seeing that Ervin was in no shape to drive.

"What was it, then?" Fatima asked. "That story you guys are telling don't make no sense." She was leaning against the bathroom doorjamb, eyeing her husband worriedly.

"I don't know," said Ervin. What he had not told his friends nor his wife was the weird dream that he had when he blacked out. He closed his weary eyes, set his head on the pillow, and pulled the covers over himself. As he drifted off to sleep, images of eldritch shores flashed in his mind. He had altogether entered an alien world.

Fatima awoke with the morning sunrise on her eyelids. She half turned to see if Ervin had gone to work.

With no bulk of a body underneath the comforter, she assumed he had woken up early as usual. She would get up and prepare for a day of work in her home office.

She observed that her husband must have slept like a rock, for she had not been awakened by his thrashing around, which he'd done the last few nights. Still, even with Ervin gone, the unmistakable sea-reek from the previous evening lingered in the air. A cold shiver climbed her spinal cord and burst in her brain. A dread intuition.

Fatima sprang up in bed. Her heart a blast-beat, she tentatively reached her trembling fingers toward the rumpled section of the comforter beside her. Grasping its edge, she moved it delicately at first. A puff of fine dust rolled out, causing her to cough. Through the dust, she could just discern the outline of an unfamiliar shape on the mattress. She tore the cover off the bed.

Embedded in the mattress itself was a rough figure of a human being. Or, rather, the skeletal form of a human being. The dark sockets of the skull were flattened against the grain of decrepit thread. Below that, anatomical lines crisscrossed in places, jutted out awkwardly in others. Barely perceptible ghosts of tissue and sinew lined their confused patterns over the entangled specimen. These were the fossilized remains of an organism crushed incredibly by compressed eons. Weighed down by the burden of concealed knowledges, petrifying truths that had overwhelmed the mind-body construct of the man once called Ervin, and the curse of consciousness he had so recently negotiated.

A shattering howl erupted from Fatima's diaphragm, rendering her throat raw and her eyes two hazy clouds. She slunk off the bed onto the floor and crept across the dusted carpet to the door. Running wildly to the garage in bare feet, she located the fishing rod leaning in the corner, that of the garage sale purchased only a few days prior. Sensing it was the cause, it was all she could think of to destroy it.

But it could not be destroyed. Instead, the rod flexed like a graceful bow in her hands. It formed a perfect arc, a horizon beyond which we were not meant to comprehend.

We Are All Merely Passengers

The line stretched on for blocks. Family members of the victims had been waiting for several hours in the stifling heat, hoping against hope that they might get the chance to identify their spouses, their sons, their daughters. They were beyond exhausted. Women's tears were dried upon their cheeks, while the crying children in their arms had not, for a long while, been fed. Men loosened the collars of their formal outing wear. The clothing of many of them were still wet from the murky water of the Chicago River.

The odor of decomposition wafted into the humid afternoon air. The makeshift morgue, which had been set up at the city armory, contained hundreds of newly-arrived corpses. The area was chaotic with panic since early morning. With so many passengers still unaccounted for, the distress of not knowing whether loved ones had perished was the heaviest curse. No one present had witnessed a joyous scene so abruptly turn to misery.

Among the waiting throng was a middle-aged man wearing a newsie cap. He had been asleep in a boarding house near the scene of the tragedy when he was awakened by the shouts of alarm outside his window. It seemed that every tenant in the building rushed out the door toward the river. Arriving at Dearborn Street Bridge, he jostled his way toward the rail to see what all the commotion was about. Craning his neck, he was stunned to see a steamship rolled onto its side. There was a multitude of people stranded upon it. Worse, there were clearly hundreds of bodies clustered thickly in the river, a fetid human stew.

Several were thrashing around, but some were motionless. He saw a woman's long air floating like her own seaweed crown. He saw a little boy floating face down in the water, his red suspenders still hooked onto the back of his short pants. He saw shirtless men jumping into the river from the street, surely in attempt to rescue the frightened helpless. It was a bedlam of splashing and gasping. Bystanders tossed random buoyant objects into the river, while police officers hauled in ropes whose ends were gripped by desperate hands.

With each passing minute the pandemonium grew. Bodies pulled with effort from the river were placed side-by-side directly in front of the wailing crowd. Some sat up and vomited, some writhed in agony, and some were as still as stone. Bellows-like contraptions were stuck into the mouths of twitching victims in an aim to provide them breath.

Recovering from his initial shock, the man in the newsie cap attempted to move closer to the site of the massive ship, but the pressing horde was dense with gaping pedestrians.

His eyes fell on a pretty woman near the bank. Her face was contorted with worry as her eyes searched the surface of the river. On her neck, the man noticed, was a set of pearls. As he watched the rings on her balled fists glimmer in the morning sun, an insidious thought entered his mind.

Now, several hours after the accident, he was waiting in the long line outside the morgue, having inserted himself into the mass of survivors and other relatives who came forth from their homes after learning of the tragedy. The nonstop clamor of horse-drawn wagons on the cobblestone streets mixed with the shouts of policemen, who were trying in vain to control the hysterical crowd. Some wagons carried supplies such as dry clothing and towels, while others carried the bodies of the recently drowned. Another open carriage was stacked with wooden coffins. The man pulled the front of his cap tightly over the perspiration on his forehead.

You can do this Royce, he thought to himself. With the sun directly above them, the wretched people continued to wait. They could not have guessed that they wouldn't be allowed inside until midnight.

"Who are looking for, sir?" The question took Royce by surprise. He was so tired and hungry that he wasn't as focused as he should have been.

"Uh, my cousin. Mary." He blurted out the most common name he could think of. The watchman ruffled through a few sheets of paper he had. Looking into the makeshift morgue building, Royce could see lanterns lit all around the perimeter of the large hall. Some were on the ground, while others were handheld. There were even a few electric lights. The odor of putrefaction was stronger than before, and there was foul quality to the scent that was no doubt augmented by the rank river water.

The watchman waved him forward. He was promptly taken aback by the devastating sight. Hundreds of bodies were aligned in rows, each with a mortuary cloth draped over it. Many coverings were the blankets, jackets, and other materials that had been hastily gathered. Men and women inside the great hall were lifting the edges of the coverings to peer beneath, a paradoxical combination of hope and terror in their guts that a loved one might be discovered.

Royce was no stranger to death. Both parents had perished in his childhood due to sickness, leaving him an orphan. His uncle James, who took him under his roof, was killed some years later in a lumberyard accident. He had also seen a drunk man kicked by a horse that was startled by a feral cat. Once, he was in a tavern when a brawl broke out between two drunkards. One of them ended up stabbing the other in the neck with a knife. Blood squirted out like spaghetti sauce onto the wooden floor.

No, Royce was no stranger to death, but this morbid display was surreal.

You can do this, he told himself again. He held his breath and lifted the corner of a corpse's sheet. It was a young woman with her eyes closed and head tilted back, as if still straining for breath above the water's surface. With her arms she clutched a baby to her chest, its eyes also closed as if napping. Its cheeks and forehead were a blue-black bruise of trauma. Royce let go of his breath and concentrated on the woman's left wrist, which was encircled by a silver wristwatch. He took a glance around and went for it. Quick and with conviction, like he was to do taught by his uncle. He was able to complete the job with one hand, and in a moment's time the wristwatch was in his pants pocket. His fingers had inadvertently brushed against the deceased infant, giving him goosebumps.

He lowered his head so as to appear appropriately grief-stricken. He paused near a pair of small heaps on the ground that he judged to be children. Their saturated shoes were caked with soot. There was a sudden scream across the hall, followed by a wail of indescribable sorrow. A woman dropped to her knees before a body as a man held her by the elbow and removed his hat.

Royce took advantage of that distraction to lift another covering and swiftly unfasten the necklace of a woman whose damp, blonde hair covered her face. Her pastel dress was streaked by grime. There was just enough light in the hall to reflect off the unfortunate victims' jewelry, yet it was dim enough to obscure his actions. By the time he made for the exit, he had three more necklaces, another wristwatch, and half a dozen rings.

Upon leaving the armory building, which was now being guarded by extra police officers, he tugged on his cap and shook his head somberly. Remarkably, no questions were asked. He also noticed that the crowd gathered outside hadn't diminished whatsoever. In fact, he heard the wheels of yet another carriage full of corpses approaching. The sound of weeping showed no signs of stopping, either, like an endless river that perversely mirrored that which had consumed so many souls.

At this hour of night, the mugginess had dwindled. He stuffed his hands deep into his pockets to muffle any possible jangling sounds, and soon passed the section of the river at which bodies continued to be recovered. He was starving. First, he would sit for a bowl of stew at his regular spot across from his boarding house on Kinzie Street. Then, he would track down Mandy. She was sure to be around tonight, as the whole city seemed to still be awake in the aftermath of the tragedy. She would certainly help him sell the purloined loot.

There was a shortcut through a narrow gangway between two squat, brick buildings on the path to his destination. Royce had traversed it countless times. There were no street lanterns near, so it was always extremely dark in that tight gangway, especially after nightfall. Rats usually scuttled out of the way up ahead of him, while the vague stink of urine invaded his nostrils as he hurriedly ambled through.

This time, however, something different happened.

The brick wall of the building to his left was windowless, but the right side featured a low, lone window. The window had been dark each and every time up until tonight. Tonight, it was lit from within, and as he neared it, Royce slowed and then stopped out of sheer curiosity and confusion.

There was a woman seated at what appeared to be a glass table. Atop it was a rectangle of electric light, emanating from a thin slice of metal like a screen. She speedily moved her fingers above another attached slab, in mimicry of the use of a typewriter, a machine Royce had seen as a kid at the World's Fair. He pressed his nose up against the window and watched black letters appearing like magic across the rectangular screen. And then images appeared like moving pictures, only in color and staggeringly lifelike.

Shuddering in illogical fear, Royce looked away. When he looked again, all he saw was darkness. What mad vision was this? *I must be truly bone-weary,* he thought. He exited the gangway and made a beeline for his apartment. His head was still spinning when he consumed half a brown apple and a piece of dry cheese. Then, fully clothed, he collapsed on his bed and fell asleep.

"You got all this *where*?" asked Mandy in disbelief.

"You heard me right," Royce said.

"Oh, I don't know, Royce. All those poor people. They're still bringing them up out of the water."

"What's the difference?" he replied. "At least these people won't never know what they're missing."

"Yeah, but what about their family? They might notice something's missing," Mandy said.

"So, it sank to the bottom the river," Royce replied. "There's plenty ways they could've lost their jewelry in that ship that turned over. Shoes, too. I saw lots of bare feet in the morgue last night."

Mandy took a sip of her black coffee. Royce found her that morning sitting at a table in the Streeterville Pub, where she was reading a house copy of the *Chicago Daily Herald.* The date printed at the top was July 25, 1915. The bold, black headline was spread across sepia-toned paper. It read: HUNDREDS DIE IN SS EASTLAND DISASTER. The astonishing photograph under the headline showed the steamship on its side, with passengers balanced upon it and numerous heads protruding above the surface of the river. The caption beneath the photograph caught Royce's eye: *The prospective joyride to a company picnic was transformed into a veritable harvest of death.*

"I suppose we could take this all to Max," Mandy said. "Probably get them sold before tomorrow."

"That's what I'm saying," Royce said. He raised himself and went to the bar, where he ordered a pork sausage and a glass of ale. "You seen Max around?" he asked the bartender.

"Too early. Maybe after lunchtime," responded the bartender. He looked Royce in the eye, and then took a quick glance over at Mandy, who was sitting at a table hunched over the newspaper. "If not, try the side door tonight." He motioned with his head toward the wall of the pub. Royce gave him a terse nod, set down some coins, and made his way back to Mandy with the sausage and beer in hand.

She was examining the second page of the newspaper, on which was printed a photograph of the bodies laid out in the morgue. She touched the picture with a tip of her finger, as if attempting to feel the heartache it contained, and looked up with a deeply concerned expression.

"Royce, this isn't right," she said.

"Well, if you don't like it, then maybe this time I'll keep all the money for myself."

Mandy frowned. "Some partner *you* are."

"Oh, is that all I am?" said Royce. He was not naive enough to believe that he was the only man Mandy went around with. He knew he didn't have the means to support her even if she consented to it. Perhaps someday, he told himself. She had been surviving the unsavory Streeterville area of town on her own for many years now, and would no doubt be offended if anyone suggested she couldn't handle herself.

Mandy waved at him as one would absentmindedly swat a mosquito.

There was something else on Royce's mind, which was the vision he experienced the night previous, or whatever it was. He decided to keep it to himself for now.

"Look, I've got to run," said Mandy. "Gotta meet some people."

"Who?" asked Royce.

"Since when do I have to report everything I do to you?" She squinted at him. "Anyway, good luck with Max. If you find him." As she walked out, Royce noticed a few heads turn toward her. He folded the newspaper and pushed it to the side. He would finish his breakfast and head back down to the river. See what other opportunities might crop up.

The site of the capsized ship was cordoned off. Hundreds of people were within the sectioned area, including police officers and men in suits. Royce observed a doctor in a white coat kneel next to a man and jab a syringe into his bare bicep. As opposed to yesterday, all the bodies lying on the street adjacent the river were motionless. A continuous stream of horse-drawn wagons arrived and departed through the masses. Royce observed one wagon donning a white flag with a painted red cross on it. He followed it with his eyes until it disappeared behind the Reid Murdoch building, a red-bricked edifice with a clock tower which had recently been built right on the river.

He realized that the Reid Murdoch was being utilized as an additional morgue, so many were the lifeless bodies hoisted from the river over the last twenty-four hours. As he pushed toward the building among the frenzied action, he saw that it was also a makeshift hospital, as doctors were shuffling into the building as well as congregating near the entrance. He felt the tingle of a thief's intuition.

A matter of minutes later, Royce was once again standing in line among the families of the hapless victims. From outside, hear could hear the wails of grief as the bodies of loved ones were discovered. When he finally got inside a few hours later, he was surprised to see so many unclaimed bodies. The heaps of the dead covered the floors from wall to wall, and the stench was insufferable. There were bulky heaps, small heaps, and all sizes in between. The Chicago River was a tributary to this Sea of Death.

Daytime thievery proved to be challenging. Sunlight flooded through the high windows, rendering the floating dust particles visible above the desolation. Nevertheless, Royce came away with a moderately-sized loot. The easiest to take were rings, as the soft skin of the cadavers allowed for smooth removal. A few bloated fingers, however, did make the task tricky. Trying to detach necklaces and wristwatches was altogether too risky in the relatively well-lit room.

"May I help you, sir?" asked a young nurse, who came up behind Royce and startled him. He thought it best to keep his head down. "No, thank you," he muttered quietly, and moved toward the exit as inconspicuously as he could.

Out in the street, Royce expected to waste no time in finding Max to negotiate the sale of his newly-acquired valuables. His mind was so focused on making money that he almost forgot about the gangway, which cut straight through half the city block. He abruptly stopped at its opening, and for a moment considered going all the way around the building. Squinting down the corridor, he figured it was childish to hesitate on account of a prickle of fear, especially during the day.

The lone window, to his dismay, appeared to be lit from within. Against all explanation, there was the woman in the room. She was running in place on a black surface. No, not quite running in place, he perceived. The strip underneath moved as she ran. The woman was looking into a light screen that was mounted in front of her. She was wearing a sleeveless shirt and short pants, a white dot planted inside her ear.

Royce took off toward the end of the gangway.

Back in the open air, he rubbed his eyes and pounded his forehead with the base of his palm. *Just what the devil is happening to me*? Reaching his boarding house, he stomped up the stairs to his second-story room. He took out a small bottle of whiskey he had been saving for a special occasion, perhaps with Mandy, and unscrewed the cap. *To calm my nerves*, thought Royce, as he threw back his head and downed the last few ounces.

He took the small pouch from beneath his worn mattress, and laid out yesterday's jewelry on the bed. He extracted today's loot from his pockets and placed it beside the rest. This ought to bring in a fair price. If only Mandy were around to go with him. She was the one who first introduced him to Max, after all. He'd always thought there was something unsettling about the man.

He gathered up the stolen items and put them into the pouch, which he inserted into his inside jacket pocket. He would have to decide whether her were really going crazy later. For now, he had business to attend to.

Royce rapped his knuckles on the heavy, wooden side door of the Streeterville Pub. There was no answer. The collective shadows of the crowded buildings loomed over the intersecting streets and alleyways. He knocked again, this time more forcefully. Royce unwittingly placed a hand over his chest and looked around warily.

"Hey there, friend," said a voice. It was a husky man in a long coat.

"Max is expecting me," said Royce, with a sudden sense of alarm.

"Well, Max ain't in," said the husky man. Two other men emerged from the shadows. One was tall, with his hands behind his back, and the other with his hands in his pockets. They took slow, deliberate steps toward Royce.

"Guess I'll be on my way, then," said Royce. He could feel the bulge inside his jacket.

"What do you got there, friend?" said the husky man, motioning with this thick hand.

"Nothing," said Royce, trying to avoid the nervousness from coloring his words. He avoided making eye contact.

"Don't look like nothing to me," said the tall man. "Maybe we can be of help to you."

"No, thanks," Royce said in a low voice. "I'll come back later to see Max." He took several quick steps as he spoke these words, but the man with his hands in his pocket pulled out a knife and said, "No reason to be off so soon."

The tall man seized Royce by the arms and harshly pulled them behind his back, locking them in a painful grasp. "Hey! Let go," cried Royce.

The husky man rifled through Royce's pockets, like he'd done this sort of thing before, and in short order located the pouch in his jacket. The man said, "I think I found a little present."

"Give that back," Royce exclaimed, before the tall man yanked his arms back further, nearly dislocating his shoulders. Gasping, a white burst of surged through his mind and blurred his eyesight. The next thing he felt was a fist slamming into his jaw. His head jerked sideways, and immediately he tasted blood.

Another crack, this time to the nose, and a warmth streamed from his nostrils. Now a brutal thump to his gut, knocking the wind of out of him. His right cheekbone smacked into the pavement. Curled into a ball, Royce gingerly opened his watery eyes to see the shoes of the three men strolling away. He heard echoes of casual laughter.

With great effort he raised himself to his knees and spat blood onto the ground. With his tongue, felt a gap where a tooth should have been. His nose was swollen. He turned to look at the heavy, wooden door, which was

the Cook County Insane Asylum on the north side of the city.

"What do you mean?" asked Mandy. "You need a real doctor to look at that face of yours."

"I've been seeing things. People, I mean, doing strange things I don't understand. And then I blink, and they're gone." Royce took a swig of his beer. "Say, you got a cigarette?" Mandy got up and procured one from her friend, who was still seated at the bench and now talking to a man.

Royce leaned over to light his cigarette on the table candle. He blew a puff of white smoke before continuing. He could see that Mandy's expression was a mixture of confusion and concern. "Not only that. I can feel another one coming. I know where to look."

"I told you it wasn't right, taking things from those poor people," Mandy said. "You're seeing odd things, I just know it has something to do with that." She crossed her arms. "There's enough living people in this damned town to keep you going, if that's what you want. Why you can't get a job in the lumberyards, I'll never know." Royce shook his head wearily.

"Go home," Mandy told him. "Get some rest. I'll talk to you tomorrow. I've got to get back to my friend over there." When she left the table, Royce exhaled the last of the smoke and stubbed his cigarette out on the ashtray.

The night air was cool. Dusk was falling, and the commotion near the river finally began to subside. The search for survivors continued, and groups of curious onlookers were gathered at the site. Journalists hungry for sensational photographs still prowled the area in numbers. There was no need for him to go through the gangway, but he wanted to. He could not articulate why, but the gut feeling inside was as real to him as the cut on his lip.

Royce was closer to the end of the gangway opposite where he'd entered previously, and he realized that the third window was situated near this end. His head swiveled back and forth to confirm that no one would see him enter the narrow space. He knew of only a few others who used this shortcut between buildings. The dim light of the fading day barely reached the ground. Proceeding a few anxious steps into the gangway, he saw that the third window was dark. His head was pounding as he approached it step by cautious step.

He was determined to see what he believed, deep down, needed to be shown. When eventually he found himself across from the window in that narrow space, he was perplexed and even a bit disappointed. Although the first two visions had terrified him, he wanted to know whether it was all in his head, or if the experiences were really somehow connected to robbing the dead, as Mandy suggested. At last, the white light of the window flickered into existence.

Startled, Royce tried to compose himself despite the pain in his stomach, face, and shoulders. There was a man and woman seated together on a soft couch, facing away from the window. They, too, were watching moving pictures on a rectangle of light, just as the other strange people had been doing. Impossibly, there seemed to be no light projector of any kind. The people in the pictures were inside motorized wagons that made extremely loud sounds, which didn't seem to bother them. Instead, they laughed and talked, all the while moving at incredible speeds around mountains and the edges of cliffs.

In a flash, the picture changed to a show a large crowd of people seated around an area of green grass so real, Royce felt as though he could have reached out and touched it. Uniformed men in caps were throwing a ball to each other. Wait, he thought, this is something I recognize. Then he looked at a sizable picture on the wall, in color as if it were cropped out of real life. It showed a radiant blue river flanked by spires of glass and shiny metal that reached into the clouds. A boat was passing through a raised drawbridge, much like the one near his own boarding house.

As Royce stared at the picture more closely, his nose up against the window, he glimpsed something that sent chills down his spine. In between so many structures of glass and metal, he saw the red brick of the clock tower. It was the Reid Murdoch building, and it was right where he saw it every day, on the bank of the filthy Chicago River. Was this his home, twisted into an alternate reality by his own mind? Or a demonic hallucination, worthy of having him committed to the Cook County Insane Asylum? The woman held a small version of the light rectangle in her hand, which she rubbed with her index finger. The man next to her held out an object at arm's length, and the rectangle screen went dark as pitch.

In that split-second moment, the man, woman, and Royce all saw the reflection in the black void of the screen. Each cried out in shock at the rotting skull glaring back at them. Strips of soft, decayed flesh hung from its cranium, along with chunks of sopping, putrid tissue. The deep-set eye sockets were empty and dark. Raising his hand to his mouth in sickened horror, Royce saw a skeletal hand mirroring his own. He then fully understood that it was *he* who was the decomposing ghoul in the reflection.

He fled down the gangway and emerged under deep red skies. With his head spinning and body aching, he heard the clamor of people and rolling carriages near the river. Street lanterns were being ignited to provide illumination to the workers clearing the disaster area. Outside the makeshift hospital, Royce witnessed a doctor kneeling next to a man lying on a stretcher, two fingers pressed to his neck. In a clear voice, the doctor pronounced the victim's condition with a mortal finality: *Gone.*

The reflection of his own eroded face wracked Royce's mind. His heart beat rapidly and his fingertips tingled from the effect of the inexplicable vision. He was at a loss for what to believe, and didn't know what to do. He wished he had another cigarette.

"Excuse me. Excuse me, sir?" Royce turned around to see a woman in a gray dress. Her long brown hair was tied at the back, and her pale skin seemed to glow in the gloom. Clearly distraught, her voice trembled as she spoke. Wringing her hands together, she asked, "Have you seen my children?"

Royce was nonplussed. Had this woman really lost her children in this area, at this time of night? He took a quick glance around before answering, "I'm sorry, no."

"They were just here," said the lady in gray, moving briskly and pointing toward the river. "Are you sure you haven't seen my children?" A peculiar odor emanated from her body, almost like the scent of sewage.

I am under no obligation to help this woman, Royce thought. Something in her demeanor was abnormal. "Please," she said, and gripped his arm with the strength of a vise. "Please help me find my little children. They were just right here," she repeated, this time definitely pointing at the river.

"What do you mean?" asked Royce. "Here in the water?"

"They were just here," she said again. "Help me find them."

Royce blinked and peered into the water. Just across was the SS *Eastland*, still on its side, the hull bulging out like the gut of a grotesque, drowned animal. "There!" cried the woman. He thought he saw movement on the surface. The woman released her grip on Royce's arm just as his shoes slipped on the slick stone bank. The cold water enveloped him like a dark, terrible womb.

Mandy was surprised not to have run into Royce all day. Maybe he's recuperating from his injuries, she speculated, or wanted to stay in because of the weather. It had been pouring rain all day, which prompted the desire for her own languid evening at the Streeterville Pub.

She took a drink from her glass, set it down, and opened the evening edition of the *Chicago Examiner.* The main headline was the fact that many disaster victims had yet to be accounted for. Inside the paper was an extensive display of closeup photographs. They were the faces of people who had been pulled from the river over the course of the last few days. Their pictures had been taken post-mortem and presented anonymously, as no one knew their names.

As Mandy was about to take up her glass for another drink, she froze. Her heart skipped a beat as she focused in on one particular face. It can't be, she told herself. There on the page was a photograph of Royce. His swollen face featured a black eye and a gash on the mouth. She could see the dark gap between the slightly parted lips. The caption below his picture read: *Unclaimed body.*

Generation

The day after my grandfather's funeral, my grandma sat me down to tell me a bizarre story about him. She had never told another soul, she said, but wanted to confide in me as her only grandchild. It was something that had been bothering her for decades, but the mixture of peculiarity and embarrassment compelled her to wait until my grandpa was safely under the ground. She felt that I should know. After all, my grandparents were the ones who had truly raised me.

"Your grandad Sal and I were on our annual trip at Woodland Dunes," she began. "You know how your grandad loved to fish." I had gone fishing with my grandpa many times, but I had no real interest in it. After casting a line or two just to make him happy, I'd crack open a can of Coke and read one of my sci-fi books. Come to think of it, my interest in strange stories is probably a reason why my grandma felt the need to relate this story to me in particular.

Grandma continued. "It was the last day before returning home. Your grandad went out to the dock extra early that morning. It was at least a few hours before sunup. He knew the area quite well, because we'd made the same three-hour drive each year around Labor Day. Well, up until that year."

"What year was that, exactly?" I inquired.

"It was 1962. I remember it well." Her voice took on a solemn tone. She shifted a bit in her living room chair. "Anyhow, it was still dark out when he returned to our cabin, which caught me by surprise. I was still in bed." I had never seen my grandmother so nervous. "This isn't easy to say, Marc. But your grandad Sal was aggressive. Very much so. Almost violent."

I was shocked. "You mean he hit you?"

"No, not that kind of aggressive. It was like he was possessed or something, when he approached me. His hair and clothes were sopping wet and he smelled like the river." I lowered my eyes to the floor as my grandmother's face flushed a darker shade. "Nine months later your father was born."

Trying to hide my discomfort, I fiddled with a frayed edged of a couch cushion. She went on after a moment. "We didn't discuss the whole ordeal until the next summer, when I brought up the fact that we hadn't yet chosen the dates for our yearly trip to Woodland Dunes. We were at breakfast, I recall. You grandfather put his fork down and glared up at me. He had a look in his eye I'd never seen before, and it chilled me. All he said was, 'Not goin' this year.'"

That sounded like Grandpa. Don't get me wrong. He was caring and supportive, but was often quite short with his words. Bluntness was his character, and he was rarely challenged by anyone around him. At least I didn't see it. Grandma went on, saying, "By that time your father was a baby of a few months, but there was no reason why we couldn't drive up to our regular vacation spot as a little family. I sort of looked forward to it, in fact. Well, anyway, I kept harping on him and finally he came out with it."

"Grandma," I said, "you don't have to continue if you don't want to." I said it so weakly and lacking in conviction that it hardly qualified as a serious comment. Inwardly I wanted to know, of course. After hearing what she told me next, it was wise she ignored my comment.

"Your Grandad Sal had just launched his little fishing boat onto the West Twin River, near where it meets Lake Michigan. It was still dark out, remember. Probably not even five in the morning yet." My grandmother furrowed her brow in storytelling concentration. "He heard it first, he told me. A rumbling sound that seemed to come out of nowhere. There was a flash directly above, followed by a streak of orange. And then there were splashes all around him in the dark waters of the river, as though it were raining small objects."

She paused momentarily and pressed her eyeglasses to the bridge of her nose. I found myself intently leaning forward as she continued. "Something hit the bottom of your grandad's tiny boat, making it sway back and forth on the calm surface. It was a loud, wet smack, he said. Those were his exact words. When he shone his flashlight on the object, he was confused by what he saw. It was a pulsing blob, he said, semitransparent. Like a lump of frogspawn. Those were his words."

"So, what was it?" I heard myself say, almost involuntarily.

"He didn't know, but, according to your grandad, the next thing he remembers, he was on the ground behind our cabin. He'd always claimed he didn't remember being aggressive with me. But there he was, on all fours, soaking wet and vomiting."

"So, was he sick, or did he almost drown, or what?" I asked. This was all new to me, and it dazed me to know how long my grandparents had kept this odd story a secret.

"Marc," Grandma resumed, "your grandad was vomiting up that stuff. It came out of him in thick globs of jelly. I saw it for myself. It had a horrible, disgusting smell. I was hysterical, because your grandad could hardly catch his breath. By that time the sun was dawning, and in the first light he went out to find his fishing equipment. The thing is though, his fishing boat was still way out on the river, bobbing up and down by itself. Meaning, he didn't come back to land by boat."

"How come you or Grandpa never said anything about this?" I asked.

"He refused to discuss it anymore, and I didn't argue with him. But I'll tell you one more thing. Your grandad had nightmares for many years afterward, and I've always suspected they had something to do with that day. He'd never had nightmares before that. I think they sort of peaked around early September each year, but that might just be me looking too deep into something that's not really there. Anyhow, when your mom and dad disappeared the nightmares only grew more frequent."

I knew about my grandfather's nightmares. My bedroom was just down the hall from my grandparents' room in the house where I grew up after losing my parents. It seemed at least once per month, in the middle of the night, that I would hear him issue a wail of utter terror. I would then usually hear the floorboards creak as he walked around the house, and the rushing sound of curtains drawn open, as if my grandad were on the lookout for someone, or something, that never came.

As for my parents, they were heading back from Michigan when their small private airplane vanished over the Great Lakes. I was only seven years old. They were celebrating their ten-year wedding anniversary with friends for the weekend. The plane was owned and piloted by my father's friend from college, whose own wife was also on the plane. The whole event was on the news for a few days, and then we all went on with our lives.

It had been an emotionally tumultuous week. My grandfather's death from advanced cancer had come swiftly, and there was comfort in that. Some friends and family who I hadn't seen in years came to the funeral, which released a flood of memories of my parents. They never had a funeral because their bodies had never been found. They had been filed under "missing."

I took the week off work on bereavement leave, and during that time I did some research online, which eventually led to my own trip north. I discovered that there was verifiable truth to at least part of my grandfather's story. While searching for sky phenomena occurring in 1962, I found a documented fireball in the early morning hours of September 5th. In fact, this event was the visible reentry of Russian spacecraft Sputnik IV, which disintegrated in the sky. A fragment crashed onto the streets of Manitowoc, Wisconsin, a city located just south of where my grandfather was fishing at Woodland Dunes.

Subsequent metallurgical analysis of the fragment had confirmed that it was indeed a piece of Sputnik IV, which the Russians had launched into orbit more than two years prior. I also encountered a few strange peripheral stories about the event, which may have been partly fueled by the strained relationship between Russia and the U.S at the time. One report in particular referenced an amateur radio operator who claimed to have intercepted audio transmission from Sputnik IV that featured indistinct vocalizations. The Russians, however, maintained that the spacecraft was unmanned.

I found a previously classified American document from January 1963 that broke down the fragment's analysis, which expert space engineers determined was consistent with an object that had been in orbit for two years. In addition, there was an unidentifiable viscous substance smeared within the joints of the scorched machine. Further testing of this uncertain substance by a team of scientists had proven inconclusive. Notably, its atomic makeup is listed as "of unknown origin."

Yet another article about the crash, this one from the archives of a local Wisconsin newspaper called the *River County Gazette,* told the story of the event on its one-year anniversary in September 1963. Several witnesses, including two police officers on duty at the time, reported a thunderous sound accompanied by an orange-red fireball. This sighting was followed by a brief rain of objects that fell with wet plops, a description matching my grandfather's. Some fell on their sidewalks, and some on the roofs of their houses. In each case, the individuals had considered it unusual, but assumed that they had witnessed the breakup of a meteor.

Apparently, Sputnik IV had brought back to earth something extra, whether intentional or not. I was determined to know more, and decided to start by making the trek to Woodland Dunes myself. With the extra days off work, I figured the three-hour drive northward along Lake Michigan would be therapeutic, with its open skies and invigorating air. It was also my way to honor my grandpa Sal's memory in some small way. At least that was my thought process at the time.

The night before I planned to drive up north, I suffered a powerful nightmare. It began with my grandfather floating toward me out of a blank white background. He was repeating a word over and over, yet his mouth was not moving. I could not quite make out what he said, which seemed to be in a language I did not recognize, or else distorted by some irregular medium. It may have been the word "grandchildren." He was wearing his fishing clothes over his frail body and sallow skin.

My feet were stuck in place, but my grandfather moved toward me until we were face to face. But it wasn't his face, not quite. The eyes were a little larger, his forehead a little wider. The browns of his irises were replaced by black voids that opened into endless gulfs, striking my dream self with vertiginous torment. His putrefied lips parted to reveal a mouth stuffed with the frogspawn substance, which he vomited forth into my own suffocating mouth. The drowning sensation became intolerable with the gelatinous intrusion up on my lungs and organs. I woke up in the dead of night gasping like a fish out of water.

The dream brought to mind an unsettling thought. There is an unnamable emotion I've experienced in certain random times throughout my life, when spontaneously I glimpsed into a mirror and perceived a face that was not quite my own. I shook off the feeling.

What I envisioned to be a therapeutic drive turned out to be miserable. I could barely keep my eyes open for the poor night's sleep, and the iced coffee I picked up did nothing to relieve my headache. To make matters worse, it rained the whole way from my apartment garage to the rental cabin in Woodland Dunes. It was a cool and damp autumn day.

My sinuses were stuffed up, and the closer I approached my destination, the more I felt pressure as though I were under water. The radio was a low, subharmonic drone to my ears. I drove past the site where my grandmother told me they used to stay, and it was clear that those cabins had been long-demolished. To my alarm, my vision began to black out as I parked the car in the gravel driveway and carried my duffel bag to the front door lockbox. I could smell the foamy, algae scent of the river and the lake nearby. There was something intangible in the air, like a forbidden kind of knowledge just beyond the horizon of cognition. But perhaps it's just me looking too deeply into something that's not really there.

They wasted no time in visiting me that night. The rain had cleared around dusk, and the clouds dissipated to reveal a near-full, waxing yellow moon above the lake. My sinus pressure had not improved much, but my senses were alert and on edge, even. I had stayed in because of the weather, but was eager to hike around the area the next day, to retrace my late grandfather's footsteps.

I spent the afternoon reading a book of short stories I brought with me. I took two aspirin, turned down the blinds, and lied down in anticipation of waking early and walking to the river in the early morning light. The moon shone its way through the edges of the window blinds, forming a perfect square of yellow light in the otherwise pitch obscurity of the room. I was mesmerized by this image when I heard a low murmur. It was the sound of a voice, I assumed, the inhabitant of a neighboring cabin out for a nocturnal stroll.

But it repeated once and then again and again in a uniform pattern. My memory couldn't help but to instantly recall my grandfather's voice in last night's dream. The vibratory register of the repetitive vocalization induced a trancelike stupor. Then I noticed the edge of the square of light disappear from the left side of the window. The moonlight was blocked by something outside. I tore off my sheet and stood up like a marionette being drawn without its consent. I glided to the window and hoisted up the blinds in one maniacal motion.

I found myself face-to-face with a humanoid being. Paralyzed by fear, I could hear its repeating word, like a chant or some cosmic prayer, though it appeared to be mouthless. It had my grandfather's eyes from the dream, which brought back the vertiginous sensation of being catapulted through the air. Only a thin pane of glass of the old cabin stood between its flat visage and mine. Thus, I could clearly hear its terrible incantation: *Brother. Brother. Brother.*

My body hitched forward, and in an instant I was at the edge of the water where the rivers meet the lake. The pang of nausea was overwhelming. That was when I realized my paralysis was not due to fear only. I could smell the body of the being behind me, a mixture of sulfur and algae. Its chant was loud and clear in my mind, and I wondered if anyone else might hear it. When my body plunged into the cold lake in the next moment, I could still hear the incantation clearly in my mind: *Brother. Brother. Brother.*

The pressure of the water, painful at first, seemed strangely more natural to me the deeper I went. The whoosh of the water muted my rapid heartbeat. My open eyes may as well had been closed, as the blackness around me seemed as endless as the depths of the being's ocular cavities. Presently, I found myself shivering in a cave surrounded by a trio of these thin, rubbery beings. It was dim, stone room with an austerity like that of a chapel. There was no light source that I could discern, but I could see the pale shadows before the slimy walls move like wet clay. The incantation grew by degrees so that all three chanted in telepathic unison: *Brother. Brother. Brother.*

One of them came ambling forward and secreted a jellylike substance from the nether regions of its body. In one quick motion it seized the back of my head with one limb and shoved the substance into my mouth with the other. I gagged, and my eyes watered as I shrieked in muffled horror. I recognized that breathing was possible, however, as if this warm gelatin were a solid form of air. I'm sure I swallowed as much as went down my windpipe.

I thrashed around violently, and in the next instant I was thrashing in bed. My mattress was soaked, as were my clothing and hair. As exhausted as I was, I decided to leave right then and there. I drove the entire way back home under nightfall in a possessed state of trauma.

The next night I had my first nightmare. I don't remember anything outside of a pair deep, black eyes like the lake under starless skies, or the vast, empty expanse between the galaxies. I went to the window and gazed out with a pressure in my chest, not unlike the yearning for long-lost family.

Tell Me Where You Goin'

The day was uncommonly peaceful out on the lake. The bulk of the work was done, and the men gathered on deck after supper as the gilt hue of dusk filled the skies.

"I don't know, Joe. This life's provided for me, but my back's suffered for it."

Joe listened with his hands upon the rail, facing out toward the approaching land. The colors of fall imbued the hilly shoreline, still a vague spot in the distance.

"Hauling copper, you mean? Haven't been at it long as you, but I don't begrudge your leaving us." Joe pulled down at the front of his cap and tucked his hands in his jacket pockets. "This being your last trip, and at the right time, just before the cold hits."

Lonnie stretched long with his hands at the small of his back. He'd been a deckhand for 39 years on the Great

Lakes, and his body told him that this would be his last October on the water. The schooner was headed west on Lake Superior toward its destination of Keweenaw, where they would resume their labor by loading their ship before taking it back down to Detroit.

"My boy's just about the age I was when I first started out. Glad he didn't become a seaman like me. No, he's getting his education, learning to write and work with numbers like I never did. World's starting to change, and I don't expect I'll be changing with it."

"Things ain't changed *that* much, Lon. All we do is go up and down these lakes moving goods for other people. Those folks get rich and we stay the same, though we're the ones doing all the work. Same routes, same cycle. Where's the way out?" Joe took a corncob pipe and a pouch of tobacco from his inside pocket.

Lonnie gave Joe a fixed looked. "That's just what I'm telling you. It's gonna be different for my Junior. You see that?" He pointed out toward a steamship in the distance. "That's the future, and there's nothing we can do to change that fact. It's a new century, and there's new kinds of rules."

Joe let out a puff of fragrant tobacco smoke, the vessel lifting lightly on the waves. He grimaced at the passing steamship. "Those guys ain't no sailors. You can get anybody to work them boats. Don't need to know a thing about working the decks, or turning a capstan, or weighing anchor. That work's for real lakemen like me and you."

"What do you think those steamers are doing to our jobs? They don't need men like us anymore." He tapped his fist against the rail. "A good old schooner like this is a thing of the past. They say we're too slow, that we cost too much to run. Pretty soon these waters will be completely empty of beauties like her. Pretty much there already. The great wings on the lakes are almost all gone."

Joe shrugged, pipe in hand. "Well, nobody knows what the future holds." He sighed. "I'll tell you one thing, though. You won't ever find me working alongside those cinder-eaters."

Lonnie looked at his friend sideways. "You say that *now*."

The orange-red sun hovered just above the horizon. It was as though dusk was taking it slow this evening, deliberately stretching out for the magnificent scenic view. The land did not seem to be any closer than it had been the last time Lonnie made note of it.

They then heard steps approaching, and some unexpected movement among the crew. It was Ray, who hurriedly told them, "Willems says were going full sail," just before Willems himself bellowed out the command. They could see his dark silhouette set against the twilight skies, standing on a box he used as a platform.

Lonnie looked around. "How's that?" he inquired of no one in particular. "There's no wind out here." The three men dutifully convened with the rest of the deckhands in preparation for a task they hadn't anticipated performing. Presently they heard First Mate Willems' authoritative voice call out, "Heave and shanty, men, heave and shanty!"

At that, they took hold of the ropes as Ray melodiously sang out: *"Captain's in the pilot house ringin' the bell."*

To which the twenty-odd crewmen responded in unison: *"Tell me, who's on the way, boys, who's on the way."*

Ray: *"Mate's on deck and he's givin' us some hell!"*

Crew: *"Tell me, where you goin'?"*

The men hoisted like an organic machine. They fell into a rhythm as one, an animate unity shaped by seasons of toil.

"Tell me, who's on the way, boys, who's on the way."

The ripping sound of the ropes could be heard in the midst of their call. The splashing of the gentle waves against the hull paralleled the rhythm of their human song. And despite the coolness of the air, sweat ran down the men's faces from underneath their caps as they worked.

"Tell me, where you goin'?"

After some minutes, it was clear that something intangible was amiss. As Lonnie had said, there was no wind. There was no movement. Even so, they continued to work and sing.

"Tell me, who's on the way, boys, who's on the way."

Captain Dixon was now standing at the bow, looking ahead toward Gull Rock. The plan was to have the lighthouse there help them navigate their final passage before landing. In the diffuse light of dusk, Gull Rock's beacon came through as a reassuring point of orientation. As the crew completed its task, the closing line of the chorus resonated over the dark blue waters.

"Tell me, where you goin'?"

The men dispersed to once again take up their tobacco or a drink of fresh water from the barrel. Joe found Lonnie observing the captain from a distance.

“The hell’s goin’ on right now?” Joe’s breathing was still heavy after the strenuous chore.

Lonnie had a troubled look in his eye. “How long’s it been, would you say, that we could see those trees?” He leaned against the portside rail and answered his own question. “Feels like a while.”

“We’re caught in some type of current, then,” said Joe. His trusty pipe was back in his teeth. He bit down hard on it.

Lonnie kept his eyes on the captain, who was looking out through his binoculars. “Now we’ve both of us been on these lakes for how many years. I’ve never seen a current like this, have you? They don’t act this way.”

“No, I suppose not.” Joe took off his cap and scratched at his beard. “So?”

Lonnie laughed uneasily. “And take a look at that lovely sunset. It could be a picture someone painted. Lord knows I’ve seen more than a few pretty sunsets in my time out here on the lakes. I know how they feel.” He could see the captain take out his pocket watch and stare at it for a long minute.

Joe took the pipe out of his mouth and pointed it at Lonnie. "You're really starting to lose it, old man."

"I know how time works out on the water, too. You know what I'm talking about. It behaves in funny ways, strange ways. After all these years, it's in here." He lightly pounded his fist against his chest. "What's going on, you say? There's no wind, there's no current, and the time is passing mighty slow."

Captain Dixon turned, walked briskly toward Willems, and signaled him into the pilot house. They evidently wished to confer with Pilot Harper about the situation. Besides a few furrowed brows, most of the crew followed orders without putting much thought into why they were doing what they were doing. But that didn't last long. Ray meandered his way to Lonnie and Joe. "If this isn't the damnedest stormfront I've ever known," he said to them.

Lonnie took a quick glance at Joe before responding. "This ain't no storm."

"What else could it be?" Ray was a level-headed, reliable deckhand whose attitude kept the crew's spirits up.

His positive energy, however, waned a tiny bit as he asked that question.

Before Lonnie or Joe could answer, there was another call from Willems, this time for the crew to gather round under the mainsail. Captain Dixon was there, prepared to address the men directly. The deck was awash with the glow of the setting sun, which had yet to reach the horizon.

The captain spoke. "It looks as though we are currently stalled. I do not mean to arrive late for the loading. Thankfully, the engineer of our *Sturgeon* had the foresight to build oarlocks onto her gunnel. That will give us some momentum before the wind picks up, which I am sure is bound to be at any moment now. We can still make schedule." As soon as the captain finished his brief speech, Willems directed the crew to unfasten the oars and to take them into position.

Lonnie thought that this whole sequence of events was bizarre. In all his career on the inland seas, he could remember only one other time he had used the oars, and that was to help navigate a rocky coast in choppy waves. Once again, Ray cried out an opening line to the crew's favored shanty: *"The mate he says no work on the trip."*

"Tell me, who's on the way, boys, who's on the way."

The oars were set, clasped, and pulled. As they dipped into the opaque waters, the *Sturgeon* continued to gently rise and dip amid the swells, though she was stagnant in progress.

"Just lay around and enjoy the trip."

The eerie quality of the work was now unmistakable. Though the crew worked at full capacity, there was an ambiguous sense of futility. The seamen's conditioned sense of direction, of directional movement over the waves, confirmed the motionlessness of their ship.

"Tell me, where you goin'?"

Captain Dixon was beside himself with frustration. He confronted Willems face to face, saying, "I do not care what you have to do to make these men get the job done, but by God, wind or no wind, this vessel will make landfall before the sun sets."

"With all due respect, Cap," began Willems, "you won't find a finer crew out on the lakes. Experienced and strong. They'd do anything for their *Sturgeon*."

Pilot Harper sensed the tension and approached the officers. He said, "I can't explain it. We're stuck worse than if her anchor were down." They were all at a loss for words. As the captain's face turned to stone, the crewmen's cadence mirrored the tempo of their pull, and the oars splashed into the water's surface together. Ray's lilting baritone rang out for another verse, and the crew responded with their chorus.

"Lake Superior's got her hold on us."
"Who's on the way, boys, who's on the way."
"Say your goodbyes and pray if you must."
"Tell me, where you goin'?"

Something shifted then. The air pressure changed, and the dusky haze grew a tad thicker. All aboard the ship felt the abrupt surge in temperature as the sun bloomed redder. Heads turned about in stupefaction, the ends of oars gripped in calloused hands.

It was at this precise moment that a thunderous boom overhead, like the violent rending of the heavens, caused every man to hit the deck with their hands over their heads. The wood reverberated underneath them as the deafening roar rumbled from sternward. They felt it in their teeth, in their bones, and in the pit of their stomachs. Never had they heard anything as loud, so close and so immediate. Except, perhaps, a bolt of lightning striking the top of the mast. Some of the men believed it must be the end of the world.

Lonnie looked up just in time to see a colossal silver-winged machine pass directly over the ship. It simultaneously struck fear and awe in his heart. The yelling and crying out of the men were drowned out by the cacophonous engines. Though the machine appeared to be floating, airborne upon some giant tuft of air, it must have been moving extremely fast, for it went out of sight in a matter of seconds.

Speechless and trembling, Captain Dixon raised himself to his knees. For a moment, everyone was equal in their wonder. From the highest officers on down to the cabin boy, they had been rendered mute, smote by an incomprehensible vision.

Tears welled in Lonnie's eyes. Somewhere deep down and impossible to articulate, he recognized the flying manifestation as a final testament to his world. The words of his comrades echoed in his head: *"Tell me, where you goin'?"*

Crewmen began to shed their jackets in the onset, unseasonable warmth of the evening. The ochre sun was an eye observing their plight, indifferent to their human emotions. They whispered amongst themselves, as it seemed oddly inappropriate to speak aloud in the aftermath of what they had witnessed. Joe found Lonnie breathing deeply, his eyes up to the sky.

"What in the devil's name- You okay, Lon?" He pointed at Lonnie's face. "You've got a good amount of blood on your mouth."

Lonnie's face was a visage of serenity, in contrast to all the rest. He brought his hand up to his face and wiped away the blood, forming a dark red smear on the back of his knuckles. "Must've bit my lip something awful." He moved toward the water barrel, followed by Joe. Lonnie took the attached ladle and poured some water over his free hand before Joe took it from him. Without a word, Joe helped by dispensing water into Lonnie's cupped hands.

Some of the crewmen were still on the floor of the deck. He saw Ray with his back against a bulwark, knees pulled up against his chest. As Lonnie wrung his hands together and rubbed the blood off his face, he walked toward the bow, where Captain Dixon's shadowy form held a pocket watch in one hand and his hat in the other. He was looking out toward Gull Rock, where the lighthouse beacon shone brighter than he'd ever seen, unbelievably bright. Blazing in a way that it couldn't possibly have been blazing with mere kerosene.

The ship barely moved in the waves. Lonnie air dried his hands, flinging bloody droplets over the rail and into the lake. The dazed men now gathered on the portside bow of their schooner to observe the impossible, which was an array of lights all along the distant shoreline. Some were blinking, while some were red or blue. Lights on all sides of the them in the water signaled the presence of other ships, but the lanterns aboard them looked light twinkling stars rather than fire. In the undying dusk, they could see points of light overhead, moving deliberately and in different directions across the dim, spectral sky. Where a gray half-moon should have been hung a slim yellow crescent.

"This is some scary shit," murmured Joe.

"No reason to be scared of the things you can't control." Lonnie's eyes were now settled on the dappled surface of the lake. "Whatever will come will come."

The *Sturgeon* lurched downward into the trough of a wave. A cool breeze carried itself over the deck, sending a shiver among the men like a vestigial note of their preternatural experience. There was a great cheer of relief. Captain Dixon took up his binoculars to gaze toward Gull Rock, whose guiding light was once again the lone point ahead. The coast was now mostly obscured by the fallen cloak of night.

The ship was at last carried forward by the billowing sails, which were enveloped by the growing darkness. The sun finally dipped below the westward horizon, and the pilot reset the course for their destination. In a few hours the men would be loading copper onto their ship, a days-long task for the crew of twenty-odd workers. They donned their jackets and settled in for the last part of the voyage, talking amongst themselves about the changing of the seasons and their hopes for the things to come. What they had seen and heard was never far from their thoughts.

For the first time ever without having a task to perform, they sang. Ray, their worthy leader, began low and steady, and at a slower tempo than usual:

"We don't mind sailin' by the light of the moon."
"Who's on the way, boys, who's on the way."
"Haul that copper and be home soon."
"Tell me, where you goin'?"

Joe struck a match and lit his pipe, a miniature glow in his hands. He and Lonnie stood together in silence, listening to the hull of their ship glide through the waves. It was a sound they had heard countless times but had never tired of. It was a moment of solace in the hardscrabble lives of the lakemen. Lonnie looked up at the panoply of constellations, and sensed a profound timelessness in those familiar stars.

The Seven Mysterious Drownings of the SS *Neptune*

It is an established fact that sailing the seas has always been a dangerous profession. The Great Lakes certainly has its own history of tragedy and associated lore. These inland seas are home to thousands of shipwrecks. The stories of these sunken wrecks are often told in conjunction with the men and women who worked on their decks, and whose watery graves pervade the cold, murky depths of the lakes.

In the nineteenth century, many of these ships hauled materials such as lumber and iron ore across the lakes. These resources were needed to support the burgeoning towns around the lakes, the shorelines of which became America's Third Coast. One particular steamship, the SS *Cheval,* ran a circuitous route between Muskegon and Chicago, carrying massive tonnages of lumber. The ship was cursed from the start.

Built in early 1841, it was scheduled to make its first voyage late that year. Unfortunately, a fire broke out on the docked ship on the night of Friday, October 22nd, damaging the port side of the hull and postponing its departure. A man who lived close to the water had spotted a luminous glow while looking out his window. A small band of volunteers saddled a horse with severe post-haste, collected all manner of kettle and jug, and rushed to the scene. Since the fire was isolated to the stern of the vessel, it was extinguished using lake water rather swiftly, and the destroyed nautical equipment was replaced.

The fire left a set of black marks on her hull that together formed the vague shape of a soaring bird. A report of the incident in the Sunday edition of the *Muskegon Register* mentioned that the horse that led the rescue brigade that night was accidentally killed when it slipped on the mossy rocks near the shore. No cause was determined as to the start of the fire. Ironically, the SS *Cheval* was originally scheduled to set out that afternoon, but its launch was postponed by the owner of the ship, Mr. Theodore Falter of Rock Valley, Michigan. He was convinced that a Friday departure was bad luck, in adherence with seafaring lore.

In the next few years, this commercial route made Mr. Falter a wealthy man. By 1844, he had purchased several more ships and was delivering lumber to the rapidly growing Great Lakes cities. In March of that year, the ship suffered another setback during a delivery. A late winter ice storm pummeled Lake Michigan, smashing the deck to pieces and shattering the windows of the captain's cabin. His logbook, housed at Grand Rapids Public Library special collections, reads: "The skies thundered. Sounded like the ferocious growl of a wild beast."

Sometime in the spring of 1846, Mr. Falter, who was then in his mid-sixties, embarked on a river boat holiday down the Mississippi River. The trip lasted more than a month, a luxury he could surely afford. The Falter Commercial Distribution Company, however, was near its end. Alas, Mr. Falter contracted yellow fever while on his excursion to the South. He died from the disease on June 20th, 1846. A physician present at his deathbed noted in his journal that Falter's "unceasing fever and vomiting" heralded his gasping last words, which sounded something like "my feline angel!" He undoubtedly must have been hallucinating. Falter's untimely demise warranted a brief paragraph in the obituary section of the *Rock Valley Journal,* which stated: "Mr. Falter's son, one Emil Falter, is expected to take over his sire's business enterprise."

Emil Falter, an only child at 32, was contacted in Chicago and informed of his father's death. Reputedly a mercurial fellow, Emil never had been interested in shipping or lumber at all. His birth records are lost, but it is thought that his mother died when Emil was in his infancy. Documentation shows that Emil inherited the Falter Commercial Distribution Company, along with its six steamers, and quickly sold them off to eager buyers of the period. His father's first ship, the troubled SS *Cheval,* was purchased by the Chicago-based industrialist Luther Willard Smith.

In the fall of 1846, the ship was repainted and renamed the SS *Neptune.* It is believed that Smith's 11-year-old daughter named the ship after she read about the discovery of the planet in a September edition of the *Chicago Weekly Citizen.* Smith wasted no time in putting his new resource to use, immediately hiring eight seasoned men to crew the ship. Its maiden voyage was to transport a cargo of beef to the growing tourist destination of Mackinac Island, located at the northern tip of Lake Huron.

Shakespeare once wrote that "Fortune showed like a rebel's whore." In the case of the SS *Neptune* and its ill-fated crew, lady Fortune characteristically showed fidelity to no one. The rebel on this occasion was the November Witch, whose early arrival that year manifestly impeded the broadening wealth of Mr. Smith. The ship was to set sail on Tuesday, November 3rd. Curiously, as the crew was preparing to set out that morning, one of the crew members never showed. It was a man by the name of Arthur Cane.

After the catastrophe out on the lake that day, Cane was tracked down by reporters to inquire about his delinquency. He obstinately refused to speak, but his wife Agatha was not reserved. She stated that on the evening of November 2nd, the night before the SS *Neptune* was to launch upon its inaugural assignment under its new guise, her husband had a terrifying vision. She awoke in the middle of the night to find her husband out of bed and at the bedroom window: "Arthur, is everything alright?" He was petrified and couldn't speak. Eventually returning to bed, he whispered, "It came from over the lake. Great furry wings. Eyes that glowed like a cat. It called me awake." Agatha told him, "It was all just a bad dream, dear." These words are taken from the *Fergus Historical Series,* published in Chicago in 1882. Mrs. Cane added that her husband thought he had seen the figure dive into the black waters of the lake.

In the morning, Arthur Cane refused to go down to the docks. The rest of the crew, which had gathered at dawn to prepare for embarking, needed to scramble for his replacement. His position was essential, for he was the cook. One of the deckhands rushed to a nearby tavern called the Pigeon, and banged on its door to awaken the owner, Mr. Asa Lyle. The half-asleep owner, who stumbled down from his upstairs quarters, reportedly stated, "I'm sorry, but my son's taken employment on a ship that's left last week. My daughter, however, is available and a good cook, too." Having no other choice if they meant to depart that morning, the crew agreed. And that's how Ms. Addy Lyle became the cook of the SS *Neptune.*

It was immediately clear that Addy could handle herself among the men. The deckhand who had fetched her from the tavern, Jess Brown, knew of Addy from more than a few whiskey-infused nights in Hardscrabble, an area now known as Bridgeport. She spoke very little, according to patrons of the Pigeon tavern, and her face was a continual hard glare of distrust. She could not read or write but could tally up bar bills in her head. She never married nor had children. One can imagine the 30-year-old Addy striding up the ship's ramp with determined confidence among the small crew. Within the first hour on open water, however, Addy knew she was in trouble in a different way. This being her first time out on the open water of the lake, she was walloped with a bout of seasickness.

Though the skies were mostly cloudy and the winds whipped sharply, Captain Marshall Baptist deemed it no cause for concern to leave at dawn toward their northeastern destination. Soon after departure, the waves grew rougher by the minute, and the going was extremely slow. Captain Baptist was straight away worried that he would disappoint his employer, Mr. Smith, who had demanding expectations. Addy with delirious with nausea in less than two hours of travel. The ship had only advanced an estimated ten miles from the shoreline, perhaps even less. The pilot of the ship, P.J. Malley, noticed Addy's illness and made a joke about it to deckhand Tomas "Tug" Winborn. Just then, a jolt of purple lightning cracked against the sky, shedding a shock of eerie light across the gray churning surface of Lake Michigan.

The vessel's bad luck had indeed not run out. A chilling blast of wind rushed in from the north, a sound like the flapping of monstrous sails, or wings. Moses Reddick, the steamer's fireman, was belowdecks at the arrival of the gale. An intense anger began to swell in him, because he had thought beforehand that the ship should have postponed their departure until after the bad weather passed. He even gathered the courage to approach the captain to suggest that, just maybe, there might be a storm brewing. Captain Baptist replied with a sneer and said, "You've got one job, boy, and that's to tend the boiler." Tumultuous waves slammed into the hull.

The lake sprayed frigid water upon the deck as the crew struggled to stand upright. Hailstones the size of fists hammered the ship, one piece striking "Tug" Winborn on the shoulder. Being a rather stout seaman, he was stunned but still on his feet. The first mate, Henry Low, was the most experienced man on the ship, and thus was the first to realize they might not make it through the afternoon. He was familiar with the swift nature of the punishing Great Lakes gales, and with that knowledge made his way through the howling winds to the engineer, Geth Schillinger. The engineer assured Low that the SS *Neptune* had the strength to withstand the tempest.

It was not to be. Captain Baptist ordered the pilot, P.J. Malley, to turn back toward the shore, hoping to either outrun the storm or to at least hold out well enough to stay afloat. Having made so little headway, this was not an unreasonable decision. By this time, Addy was lying on the deck in a bilious daze. The brief spell of hail had ceased, but now the onset of blowing snow reduced visibility to virtually zero. The extreme pressure of one particularly violent wave cracked the hull, a blow from which the ship would not recover. On its first anniversary, the *Chicago Daily Tribune* ran a story of how this memorable storm, which is memorialized as "The Big Squall," destroyed over forty other vessels of various sizes in the south part of the lake.

At nightfall, the seven men of the crew would be safely on land, albeit drenched and exhausted. Their hair, beards, and clothing were crusted with ice, their mouths filled with a mixture of sand, snow, and mud. But what of Addy Lyle? As the crew crawled out of their lifeboat, there was nary a sign of the cook. The story that the crew subsequently told would be strange and incomprehensible. It was first told to the small crowd that gathered near the wharf. When the storm began to die down, the floundering ship was spotted by a teenage boy out surveying the damage with his dog. The boy, known only as Melvin, told the *Tribune* that he first noticed a ship very low in the water. Then, he described, he "saw a little dot out there. A speck being tossed about by the waves." It took the lifeboat approximately three hours to get back to land. Captain Baptist was the only one who did not help row back to land, as his station precluded it.

According to mate Henry Low, it was the most sudden and swiftly developing storm he had ever experienced in his 27 years on the lakes. After a mad scramble to turn the ship around, and a battle against the elements, the SS *Neptune* hit a sandbar about 300 yards out. Amos Reddick heard the tear of the hull and the water rushing in, which to him was the inevitable conclusion of his own warning. It was said that engineer Geth Schillinger was utterly awestruck at the development. He was so bewildered on the sinking ship that "Tug" Winborn was forced to literally drag him to the edge of the deck, impairing his shoulder even further. At this point, the only lifeboat on the ship was lowered at the command of Captain Baptist. It was designed to hold at least twelve people.

According to the crew members' account, the swirling snow and fierce spray rendered visibility extremely poor. Still, what happened next is puzzling. A long, penetrating wail went up from the deck. It was Addy's call of distress. Allegedly, Jess Brown went to her and took to a knee, hoping to coax Addy to her feet. He later claimed that ice had crusted over her long hair and clothes, but what most disturbed him were her eyes. They seemed to be watching something above the ship, gazing with intense exhilaration. The look on her face was a mixture of revelation and fear. Brown turned up toward the dark clouds just in time to see a shadowy form vanish into the heavy weather.

Brown, admittedly terrified, made his way across the undulating deck to fetch anyone to help with Addy. To his surprise, Winborn, Low, and Schillinger were already in the lifeboat. Captain Baptist and the pilot Malley were still at the helm when Brown called out to them, but his voice was absorbed by the winds. They abandoned their places directly and prepared to lower the lifeboat for boarding. They apparently had forgotten about Addy, or else did not care. As the ship began to sink, Reddick was seen attempting to pull Addy by the arms, but the effort was made arduous by the tossing ship and icy surface. Then he realized that the rest of the crew was leaving without him. Dropping Addy's arms, he quickly trudged his way across the slippery deck and jumped into the small boat.

Before they reached the shore near 31st street, the majority of the SS *Neptune* was already beneath the waves. Only the top of the stack protruded from the dark waters. More locals crowded onto the shore, bringing blankets and hot tea for the men. Several knew Addy from the Pigeon, and as they talked among themselves, the fact circulated that she was hired by the ship early that morning. To their shock, she had not arrived with the men on the lifeboat. Shock turned to alarm, which then turned to fury.

They demanded to know what happened to Addy. Each man deferred to the captain, who stated: "We regret to declare that the unfortunate lady was deceased at the time of the accident." The men, who had been drearily recovering from their harrowing escape from the ship, suddenly seemed a bit livelier. They dodged questions about Addy's fate, citing a desire to return to their homes or to find a doctor. The captain commented that he needed to seek out Luther Willard Smith, the owner of the ship. Within a few days, each of the crewmen had absconded to elsewhere. They left a grieving father, and a small community, with unsettled emotions and unresolved questions.

The first drowning happened less than a year later. The victim was Henry Low, the oldest and most experienced crew member, age 57 at the time of the shipwreck. He immediately was able to find new employment after the SS *Neptune* calamity, this time on a merchant ship out of Manitowoc, Wisconsin. In August of 1847, he was working on the SS *Menomonee,* when a load of iron ore never arrived at its destination of Duluth. It was guessed that the crew of sixteen were all lost to a sudden and apparently fleeting storm. Strangely, though, no storm in the area was ever reported. The ship was not seen by any other passing vessels, and no wreckage was ever found. It was as if a fracture in the wall of physical reality had opened up and swallowed the ship whole.

Several of the bodies did eventually wash up along the shore of Michigan's upper peninsula. Scavenger birds usually alerted citizens of a new dead body, and for a time buzzards were as common as gulls. The *Door County Gazette* printed a list of crew members over a period of weeks, where Henry Low's name was eventually printed. It was noted that his bare chest featured a burned image of what appeared to be a mysterious flying creature, though the family had never known him to possess a tattoo.

The second man to drown was engineer Geth Schillinger. Only in his late thirties at the time of the SS *Neptune*'s sinking, those around him said he seemed far older after the experience out on the lake, as if he were imbued by an ancient spirit. He was a changed man in other ways, too. Previously known as an intelligent, inventive sort who was always fixing things and solving problems on the job, he was afterward consumed with collecting rocks and shells. Not for geological study, however. He was convinced that there were special specimens that would complete a vast unknown puzzle, a portion of which he kept on the floor of his small second-story apartment on Madison Street.

In the early morning hours of March 30, 1852, his neighbors reported hearing him roar loudly, swing open his door, and stomp down the stairs. He was last seen near the north side of Michigan Park, where a watchman spotted a man in his nightshirt fitting Schillinger's description walk directly onto the rocky beach and into the lake. The man completely submerged himself but kept on walking, his arms outstretched as if embracing some phantom of the icy depths.

The third drowning took place eight years later. At that time, Captain Marshall Baptist was a wealthy, retired grandfather. On the night of September 7, 1860, he was on the *Lady Elgin* with his son Claude as it set out from Chicago to Milwaukee. Most passengers were on their way back home, having come to the Windy City for a political rally. The return trip was more of a pleasure cruise, with music, dancing, and drinking. Baptist and his family had built their riches on the shipping industry, and the unjust fate of Addy Lyle was an altogether forgotten thought. But on this night, the memory of the lake would seal his doom.

While the party was going strong deep into the night, storm clouds gathered over the ship. The rain and thunder did not dampen the spirits of the merry revelers. That is, until a shocking jolt portside caused chandeliers to come crashing down and sent dancers sprawling across the floor. The ship was struck by the schooner *Augusta,* and hundreds of lives were lost near Winnetka. Baptist's son survived, but the recollection of his father's death haunted him. He told the *Milwaukee Sentinel* that, the night before the accident, he had a strange dream. He recounted: "A man with a trident was seated at a table, and an ethereal being with long hair served him a platter of writhing crayfish."

The fourth man who drowned was Percy James "P.J." Malley, officer for the Union in the Civil War. His directive was to pilot gunboats up and down the Mississippi River for Ulysses S. Grant's army. In May of 1865, Confederate leader Jefferson Davis was captured in Georgia. As Union forces drew close, it was rumored that Davis and his cabinet were carrying a veritable treasure of gold. Nonetheless, there was no sign of this alleged treasure at his arrest, and thus the legend of the confederate gold was born. P.J. Malley was one of those treasure hunters who in the aftermath of the Confederate dissolution sought to discover the fortune that was unaccounted for. When Malley heard that Jefferson's treasure supposedly made it to the north, and that Union officers somehow lost it on Lake Michigan, he realized that no one was more qualified than he was to recover it.

He hired the schooner *Green Heron* out of Traverse City and enlisted a group of Potawatomi men for the mission. They set out on a cool September morning. The vessel was never seen or heard from again, another apparent victim of lakes. A recovery effort made in 1979 did find a sizable chest at the bottom of the lake, near a depth of about 200 feet. Expert divers of the *Great Lakes Shipwrecks Alliance* were able to pry it open, only to find a very old sailing cap with a simple M monogram. Floating beside it was a golden spoon.

Jess Brown, the youngest of the crew at 28 when the SS *Neptune* floundered, was the fifth man to drown. After his death, a friend confided that he sometimes spoke of that traumatic day. When in his cups, which was often, a dark pall would shade his countenance as he told the story of helpless Addy. As far as can be discerned, he was the only man of the crew to talk about the wronged woman. The source of these remarks is the 1897 book *Amazing Tales of the Great Lakes*, published in Printer's Row by Donneberry Press. He is also the only man not to have left the employment of Luther Willard Smith. He worked the lake's shipping industry as a deckhand for many more years, even after Smith sold his company to a faceless conglomerate. That's why it was bewildering to Brown's friend, known as Floyd H., that he wished to go out fishing the next day after arriving from a backbreaking weeks-long excursion on the job.

So, they launched a little fishing boat on July 9th, 1867. Floyd grew uneasy as Brown rowed the boat out toward the site of the shipwreck. Other vessels of all types were out that fine, warm morning. The two men cast their lines and waited for approximately half an hour when Brown abruptly stood up and pointed: "There's someone in the water!" Of course, there was no one there. Before Floyd could protest, Brown dove into the calm water. He did not resurface. When the devastated friend finally reeled in his line, he found at the end of it an impossibly frozen lake trout.

Moses Reddick was the sixth man to drown when he was taken by a rogue wave on the north shoreline of Rock Island. Although little is known about this bizarre incident, there are a few alleged witnesses who recounted their testimony to the Wisconsin Lighthouse Historical Society many years later. As it happened, Reddick was then working in the fishing industry, casting nets for perch and walleye in the upper regions of Lakes Michigan and Huron. His schooner, called *Pride,* was caught out in a hazy fog on the morning of May 2, 1869. Luckily, the captain knew that nearby Rock Island featured a lighthouse that for the previous thirty years had lit the way for numerous boats in that area, which was prone to unexpected fog.

As the *Pride* neared the harbor, visibility was low. There was no rain, but the craft was enveloped by a ghostly white vapor. Just before landing, Reddick looked back out over the lake, when he saw a great sailboat emerge from among the mist, gliding slowly and soundlessly. Squinting, and in a state of disbelief, Reddick saw a woman on the bow, whose long hair was plastered down as if soaking wet. He claimed that the figurehead of this spectral ship was that of a lion with wings. He had barely set foot on the beach when a massive wave came out of nowhere and swept Reddick into the lake. Since he was an expert swimmer, it can only be surmised that a rip current withdrew him toward his aqueous tomb.

The seventh and final man of the crew to drown was Tomas "Tug" Winborn, by all accounts an unjustifiably arrogant man. He got his nickname when he was a brawny teen. For a few pennies, he would single-handedly pull boats onto the lake for families out for a leisurely day of sailing. He was hired and fired from several other jobs since the sinking of the SS *Neptune.* Employers could not stand his lazy attitude or his harassment of coworkers. Winborn also walked off a few jobs when he felt he was not paid enough, or when he just got bored. In the summer of 1871, he got a job on a Chicago Sands lumberyard. On the evening of October 9, yard workers smelled smoke from coming from the south. Swiftly thereafter, the yard caught fire and spread so quickly that dozens of workers were trapped. The only escape from the heat and smoke was into the lake, so that's where they went.

Little did Winborn know that most of the town was in flames, and therefore help could not be expected to arrive. A reporter for the *Chicago Evening Post* wrote that the city that night appeared to be "the adamantine bulwarks of hell." Up to their chins in the water to avoid the hot sand blowing all around them, the magnificent and terrible glow of the conflagration rose up beyond the burning lumberyard. Directly, the frantic workers heard a distant rumbling, approaching quickly but difficult to ascertain. From out of the smoke leapt an army of horses, some aflame, crashing into the water and screaming in agony. Three days later, with the city in embers, Winborn's corpse washed ashore. It was concluded that he had drowned, but not before being kicked in the temple by a crazed horse attempting to escape the inferno.

Over the years, a few attempts have been made to recover the SS *Neptune* shipwreck. Each time, sustained inclement weather conditions prohibit any success at doing so. Funding is scarce, and the lakes do not give up their secrets so easily. The purpose of this essay is to shed light on some of those secrets. The cruel death of Addy Lyle is but one tale in which selfishness and cowardice break through the fabric of the seamen's pact. The point is not to disparage worthy seamen throughout the ages, but rather to present one crew's fragile desperation, and the tribulation that followed. Why and how these men met their ends can only be known to the spirits of the gloomy depths. Addy's story is forever lore of the lakes. Where ghost ships appear from the fog and the bones of sailors lie within her ice water mansion.

The Call of the November Witch

Soon after he survived the shipwreck, Geth Schillinger began to see visions. At first, he thought they were brought on by a lack of sleep, but they increased in frequency even after being granted the rare respite of slumber. His visions consisted of seashells arranged into linear patterns. They were not hallucinations exactly, but designs he clearly saw in his mind's eye. Like waking dreams.

With a pencil, he drew the cryptic patterns on sheets of paper he found at his workplace. The more he drew, it seemed, the more the visions would appear. First a few times per month, and then almost weekly. At any time of day or night, he was haunted by images of shells, usually manifesting themselves in curiously methodical lines.

His supervisor at the lakefront lumber yard, Hack Jarrett, discovered Geth's obsession on All Souls Day in the year 1851. The men on the graveyard shift were sharing a bottle of whiskey on a cold, clear night when Hack stumbled upon Geth at a makeshift desk of wooden cartons. An oil lamp hanging from a low rafter burned hazily over his bent form in the surrounding darkness. A frigid winter wind blasted inland over Lake Michigan, whistling through the nooks and crannies of the lumber yard.

"Geth, is that you?" asked Hack, though he knew it was him.

"Mr. Jarrett? Yes, it's me. I was just, ah, finishing up some of the records for the end of the year report. For the fall, I mean." Geth was an assistant building engineer on the yard. His lanky figure and unruly hair and beard were visible as a black shadow when he began to roll the paper into a scroll. There was a time, not too long ago, when Geth's hair and beard were always impeccably groomed, and the lenses of his spectacles clear of smudge.

"That don't look like numbers to me," said Hack, advancing slowly. "You an artist, Geth? Can I see them pictures you made?"

The supervisor was intrigued by his assistant, who had been on the job since the previous winter. Still, he knew almost nothing personal about Geth. He could tell he was smart as a whip, and knew how to fix anything. Still, the rest of the men on the night shift were inclined to avoid Geth whenever possible. He was socially awkward and tended to recede into the background of any gathering, whether it be lunchtime or the daily floor meetings.

Geth hesitantly handed over the half-rolled sheet. He bit his nails nervously as Hack looked over his drawings. There were shells of various sorts organized into spirals and rows. Shaded shapes covered the sheet. The precisely formed images were in direct contrast to their disheveled creator, as if the quality of order had shifted from his own person onto the page.

Hack's eyes widened. "What is this?"

Geth pushed his hands deep into his pockets. "Mussels, mostly." His voice rose in excitement. Embarrassed, he swallowed before quietly adding, "And lake snails. Those're harder to find." He brought forth from his pocket an assortment of his recent findings. Some shells were whole, others broken and jagged. He picked out a fully intact shell with two fingers and held it up to Hack. His supervisor narrowed his eyes at the specimen, looked back at Geth, and nodded his head slowly. "Here you go," said Hack, handing back the sheet of paper.

Hack remembered Geth's first day on the job, which is when he learned from the other workers about his troubled past. Geth had been one of the crewmen on the ill-fated steamship SS *Neptune,* which sank off the coast of Chicago in a ferocious gale in 1846. At the time of the sinking, there was a great local hullaballoo about the event. Hack recalled that seven men had survived the wreck, but the lone woman on board had gone down with the sunken vessel. Hack sought out a man who had been on the job for a long time.

"Hey, Lewis," he said, motioning for him to come close. "What was the story with the woman from that shipwreck? You know, the one where Geth was engineer?"

Lewis looked at Hack with a glint in his eye. "Nobody knows the real story. But according to people who were there when the lifeboat came in, the poor lady could've been saved. Why she didn't come in with the others is a mystery." He turned around to face the obscure waters of Lake Michigan. "Her body washed up on shore some days later. Drowned. Which means, left behind and left alive." As if in response, the marine gusts howled in intensity.

Hack silently wondered what role Geth may have played in that mystery. There was an unreasonable urge gnawing at him. Perhaps it was because of his own early calling to the inland seas that he felt sympathetic toward Geth, who now apparently lived a cursed life. Unbeknownst to most of his workers, Hack's teen years were spent hauling lumber throughout the Great Lakes. That was before his late uncle brought him onto land to work the yards.

If Hack's memory served him well, most the crew members of the SS *Neptune* fled the city to avoid the wave of accusations and interrogations. Not Geth, however. The real question was why he had remained in the city. Hack was determined to seek out the answer.

The crackling fire in the hearth radiated a comforting warmth. The River Mud Tavern was providing its patrons with a sanctuary against a biting winter evening. Hack held up his thick glass of ale as a humble toast to Geth.

"It's been near a year since you started working for me," Hack began, "but I don't know much about you." Geth stared back at him with bewilderment. He couldn't fathom why his boss wanted to buy him a drink after work. They hardly talked, other than Hack giving him instructions to repair a hole in the outside fence or to replace the wheel on a wobbly wheelbarrow.

Lately, Hack noticed that Geth was becoming even more withdrawn than usual. He often came into work wearing the same clothing for several consecutive days. A few times, Hack had noticed the back of Geth's coat and pant legs dusted with sand, as if he had slept on the beach. Returning rather late from his lunch hour one day, Hack was obliged to confront him about it. He decided not to say anything, however, when he observed that Geth's pockets were bulging. Slimy green seaweed protruded from them and clung wetly to his pants.

"Look, I know we ain't exactly friends," said Hack. "But I'm seriously beginning to be concerned about you." There was conflict in the back of Hack's mind. Was it an altruistic concern for Geth's wellbeing, or the potential decline of on-the-job production that bothered him?

Geth lowered his gaze to his glass of beer, which remained untouched on the dark wooden table whose surface was slashed with knife markings. The names of tavern customers going back a generation were etched and preserved there.

Hack realized that he needed to try a different approach. "Tell me more about your drawings," he said. Yes, that did the trick, thought Hack, as Geth reflexively raised his chin.

"See, they are not just drawings," said Geth, his voice a heavy whisper. Hack leaned in to listen in the din. The room was full of boisterous men celebrating the end of their backbreaking workweek.

"They are the pieces I must hunt for on the beach, and sometimes in the water, or in the snow," Geth continued. "They are part of a giant puzzle. I didn't realize this at first, but now it is all very clear in my head. And on the walls."

Hack paused his beer glass at his lips, just about to take a swig. "The walls?"

"My walls, yes. You see, first they come to me in something like a dream, but while I am awake. They disturb me until I draw them, and when I do it's a relief. A purge. Then I need to go find them. The mussels, the snails, sitting there among the sand and driftwood. Geth suddenly frowned, and resumed the spacey appearance he displayed earlier. Perhaps he had said too much.

Hack was transfixed, however. Too him, Geth was obviously deranged. A reliable and skilled worker, Hack thought, but not in complete possession of his faculties. If Geth wasn't careful, he'd end up in one of those workhouses for the insane that were popping up in cities all around the country, including Chicago.

At the same time, Hack didn't consider Geth dangerous. In fact, he had grown to depend on his mechanical adroitness at the lumber yard. He took a long pull of ale, but Geth still hadn't touch his own glass. The fire was getting to be uncomfortably warm.

"So, you draw them on your walls?" prompted Hack.

"Not quite," replied Geth. "I can show you."

Hack didn't know what to make of this development. He was curious but slightly unnerved. Geth raised himself off the bench and put on his scarf and cap. Before he could react any other way, Hack did the same, but not before he downed the last ounce of pale beer at the bottom of his glass.

It was a short walk to Madison Street, but the two men were shivering by the time they reached Geth's apartment building, ice forming on their beards. Geth reached into a pocket. For an instant Hack thought he would extract another shell, but it was merely a door key.

He jiggled the key in the rickety door as a freezing blast of wind raged through the street from across the dark surface of the lake. Whitecaps on the choppy waves were just barely distinguishable under the yellow light of a waxing moon. The dark waters churned under eddying gusts. The roofs of the crowded buildings rattled like rotting teeth in a vast, cackling mouth.

A steep staircase met them in the cramped foyer. The crying wail of an infant could be heard from somewhere inside the building. Taking the stairs two at a time, Geth's footsteps echoed in unison with Hack's rising pulse. Geth fumbled around to find the right key in the darkness. Upon entering the dim loft, he ignited several lamps set upon the floor. Geth was as eager as a little boy about to show his companion a new toy, but Hack immediately saw that the occasion was anything but playful.

Shells covered the walls in a stunning display of ritualistic order. Meticulously aligned mussels of dark and light shades were apparently glued athwart the ceiling as well, here and there juxtaposed with shards of their underside luminosity. Each nautical object reflected the lamplight like glimmering points across a night sky, as if the room were an astronomical microcosm. At a glance, Hack failed to discern a method to the madness, though obliquely he sensed a labyrinthine superstructure. The arbitrary architecture within the sand had been removed from the natural world and reorganized by Geth's obsessed consciousness.

The distinct scent of lake water permeated the tiny apartment, a sulfurous aroma along with seaweed and copper that filled Hack's nostrils. The floors were damp with a slippery residue. Buckets of cracked and discarded shells were pushed to one corner of the room near a stepstool. Hack was at a loss for words. A shudder rippled through his body as the wind battered the windows.

Geth pointed to the center of the room, where the paths of his beach collection converged upon a single empty point about the size of a dinner plate. "The puzzle is almost complete," he said, "but it is yet to be revealed what goes right there."

It was only a short matter of time before the troubling revelation.

The final vision came to him early one blustery morning. As Geth closed his eyes to splash cold water on his face at the bathroom basin, the outline of a large shell appeared in his mind's eye. Concentrating on the image that seemed to float before him like a shadowy phantasm, he instantly knew its significance. It was the final piece of the puzzle. His mysterious design, which wound like a magic circle inside his home, would soon be complete.

Directly, he sat down at his desk, took a sheet of paper from a flimsy drawer, and grabbed a pencil. He was so resolute in his task that the fact he had to report to work that morning was pushed out of his mind. A tempest over the lake formed as he toiled. Syncopated flashes of distant lightning among the blackening skies attended the howling winds.

Tracing the contours of his inner vision, Geth realized that this was no ordinary shell. He would draw it and then head to the beaches to hunt for it. This process had never failed him. Still, a steady consternation grew inside him as the form of his sketch emerged in greater detail.

Deep into his linework, one end of the shell resembled the curvature of a jaw that swooped down to a point and returned up the other side. The shading near the top of the sketch included two circular figures symmetrically opposing one other. His hand seemed to be controlled by an invisible agent, one to which he could only surrender. Moving again toward the lower part of the drawing, there arose a line of parallel marks separated by a thin horizontal shadow. Teeth. Why would a shell have teeth?

Geth staggered out of his chair at the stupefying import of his sketch. The legs of the chair screeched across the wooden floor. He recognized this vision—the hard jawline, the deep-set eye sockets, the gap between the two front teeth. He had seen these features innumerable times staring right back at him in the mirror. It was a vision of his own skull.

Since the time of the shipwreck about five years prior, Geth felt like a haunted man. He had planned to escape the area, like most of his fellow surviving crewmen, but the visions detained him to this rapidly growing town. Unable to find stability, he hopped from job to job at manufacturing plants and building construction sites over those years. He left most of these jobs uneventfully, sometimes wandering off toward the lakefront without returning.

And he had vowed never to work a steamship again. He had barely survived the sudden gale that was legendary on these lakes. Sailor lore claimed it was the November Witch, but she would strike during any season she pleased. He had escaped her sibilant grasp, but her dark clouds had never ceased to follow him like a hex. Geth's acquaintances knew him only as the thin, bespectacled, troubled man who was once almost swallowed by the lake.

Outside the lumber yard, Lewis spotted Geth's unsteady, ambling approach. He sought to inform Hack straightaway. Hack waited to meet Geth at the entrance gate, where he stood amid the harshly blowing snow.

"Where were you—" Hack started to say, but Geth did not stop and instead unexpectedly brushed past him. Hack was nonplussed, unsure how to react. As usual, he was unnerved by the bizarre indifference of Geth Schillinger.

That chilly, overcast day, Geth went about performing his duties. The sun set early, and the gloom invaded the city as his final vision invaded his mind. It occurred to him that he might substitute another type of skull for his own, for he could not see past the impossible conundrum of how the design could be completed. And then what? Was it a deity or a demon that called him toward the beaches?

He recalled having seen a feral cat prowling about the lumber yard. Sightings of this black feline usually occurred around dusk. He would stalk it tonight for its eventual transmutation into a sacrificial totem. He hoped it would be satisfactory.

After his shift, Geth bought a pint of milk at a nearby general store. From his coat pocket, he withdrew a tin saucer he brought from home and poured a small amount of milk. He crouched down and waited outside the fence among the shadows, near the area in which he usually spotted the cat. After a long while, Geth was startled by a pair of glowing eyes. The cat had sneaked up on him, as if summoned out of thin air. A fierce wind had been conjured by its presence.

Geth whispered, "Here kitty. Here is some nice milk for you." The cat skulked toward Geth suspiciously. "Yes, that's it. Here you go." He placed the tin saucer of milk on the wet snow. In the weighty darkness, Geth saw the impressions left by the cat's paws on the pure snow as it approached. His hands tensed, his pulse quickened. The cat paused in midstride, seeming to have sensed an insidious shift in the cold night air.

At that moment, Geth lunged forward and seized the cat around the neck with two hands. There came forth the briefest hiss before its windpipe was squeezed shut. It wildly scratched and clawed at Geth's forearms, but he closed his eyes tightly and held on. Hot tears rolled down his cheeks and were immediately frozen. His eyeglasses fogged up as the cat began to convulse violently.

Then he let go. "I can't do it," he sobbed aloud, plopping himself down heavily against a brick wall. The black cat sprinted away into the darkness, leaving the tin saucer spinning on its edge. Spilled milk endarkened the soft snow.

A short while later, Geth was wretchedly climbing the steep stairs to his apartment. His head hurt, and a wave of nausea hit him at the top of the stairs. A vision of swirling shells appeared like a sudden storm. Like the squall on Lake Michigan that had wrecked the SS *Neptune.*

Within the apartment speckled with his collection, exhaustion overcame him. Geth had scarcely slept or eaten for days. With no energy left to combat his new vertiginous vision, he laid himself on the damp floor. Virtually hopeless, an idea struck him.

He slid his body toward the epicenter of the labyrinthine structure and positioned his head neatly into the empty central space on the floor. Particles of sand were swept into his hair and beard. He stared at the ceiling as the room spun around him. Then he heard the voice. It was close, and it uttered a single word: *Geth.*

It was the thick, warbly voice of a woman. Its low register vibrated through his head. He was familiar with this sound, for it was the sound of a voice under water. As a child, he had dunked his head under the surface of the lake and screamed, feeling the bubbles emerge from his mouth and listening to the muted sonic effect made by his vocal chords. The haunting voice that called to him, however, was a perverse inversion of his memory.

He issued a bellow from the pit of his gut, ultimately grasping that the final piece of the design must be accompanied by a final act. A labyrinth is made for following after all, and it leads unicursally to one innermost destination.

Standing up, he went to his buckets and scooped up of handfuls broken shells, stuffing them into the pockets of his pants. Perhaps some fish bones and rocks had been tossed into the sandy mix, as well. He threw open his door, stomped down the stairs, and burst into the freezing night wind. Heading east on Madison Street, he soon reached the dismal shore and kicked his shoes off onto the rocky beach.

He took a deep breath of the crisp lake air and looked out across the seething black waters. The gale was fullest now, watering his eyes and vigorously blowing back his hair and beard. The blurry moon, obscured by low clouds, was dimly reflected on the rough surface. Geth sensed a paradox of dread and relief. He took a step into the icy water, which sent a chill up his spine and into his skull. Reaching out to steady his balance, he continued until waist deep, then neck deep, and then further in. Foam gathered around his body like a ghastly embrace.

The last thing Geth heard was his own warbly scream in the thick, murky dark. His lungs were paralyzed as they filled with the black blood of the lake. He was called, and so he had finally returned. This was where he belonged.

Salvaged Potency

Chicago: Present Day

When they pulled the wrecked car out of the icy river, detectives were unsettled, if not vexed. Algae covered its entire body, and stringy weeds choked the engine under the hood. The interior was smeared with a slimy coating. Although it had only been a day since the accident, the vehicle's condition was one of having been submerged for a far greater duration.

The drowned bodies inside were those of a married couple named Leon and Amanda, and they were on their way home in a winter storm when their tires hit a nefarious patch of black ice. Unbeknownst to the recovery team, a rare bottle of whiskey lied submerged in the mud beneath the shards of the shattered windshield.

On the frigid morning of the previous day, a wooden crate enclosed by rusted chains had arrived in Leon's sister Iris' condominium mailroom. It had arrived just in time for her brother Leon's one-year wedding anniversary dinner. Iris had been scrolling through an auction house's social media page in search of an extra special gift for her brother and his wife when she saw the unusual flyer. It announced an event featuring obscure items from a mysterious oddities collection that was discovered at an abandoned estate in Wisconsin. She entered the bidding and won a rare item at a not-too-unreasonable price.

Iris carried the box into the elevator and up to her high-rise unit, where she wrenched open the crate. Cradled within a boxful of musty, old newspaper pages was the aged bottle of whiskey. According to the backstory typewritten on the attached laminated index card, the bottle was salvaged from the SS *Regina* shipwreck at the bottom of Lake Huron. Perfect, thought Iris. Exactly the kind of gift that her brother would appreciate, and one that she sincerely hoped would help mend the sour relationship with her sister-in-law Amanda.

Iris excitedly called her fiancé Roman to tell him about it. He would pick her up at six, he said, to meet Leon and Amanda at the downtown steakhouse located right on the Chicago River.

Iris looked westward out of her window over the bleak, wintry cityscape. For a blink of a moment she thought the city resembled a sepia-toned postcard from the past. Brick streets, horse-drawn carts, shipyards just below. Iris shuddered with a sense of foreboding she couldn't quite place.

"Where did you find this?" Leon asked with a real sense of wonder. He turned the bottle toward the light. A silver ribbon, placed there by his sister, shone compared to the thick, lackluster glass.

"Thought you might like it," replied Iris. She looked at Amanda, whose lips were shaped into an uncomfortable smile. I don't know what I ever did to her, thought Iris.

"Well," said Roman, pointing at the bottle, "you going to open that up so we can have a taste?" All through dinner he had been trying his hardest to alleviate the tension that permeated the air. Where the unspoken enmity had originated, he had no idea. "Leon, it's whatever you want, it's your bottle."

They all turned instinctively at the sound of freezing rain striking the window. The pane of glass next to their table was a reflective black square, the icy precipitation becoming visible as it stuck in places like puncture wounds in silhouette of glass flesh.

Leon glanced at Amanda, who shrugged her shoulders dismissively. "Isn't that whiskey too old to be drunk?" Roman couldn't hold back a chortle before stifling himself.

Leon spoke while admiring the smooth contours of the bottle with its raised lettering on the glass. "Whiskey doesn't get… old."

"Well, how am I supposed to know?" said Amanda. Just as she finished speaking, a crackling sound shot through the upscale restaurant. All the bulbs ensconced in the elaborate fixtures on the ceiling glowed blindingly for an instant before burning out with a pop. Diners at several of the white-clothed tables screamed. Then all was pitch black.

Presently everyone's eyes adjusted to the darkness. Cell phone flashlights lit up the room. A blast of wind yowled violently against the floor-to-ceiling windows. In an unexpected reversal, they had now been transformed to lenses through which the wild outside world was made clearer. Peering out, the two couples saw that visibility was reduced to nil by the blowing snow.

"Temperature must have dropped," stated Roman. His voice took on a note of gravity that was not previously present.

From the entranceway came the bold voice of the restaurant host. "May have your attention please." The nervous chatter subsided. "We have contacted the electric company, but it seems our entire area is without power. Please remain calm, and we will update you shortly."

"Seriously?" said Amanda. "What kind of place is this?"

"It's not their fault," countered Iris. Then Leon cut in, perceiving the rising strain between his wife and his sister. "That's true. The forecast wasn't this bad. Couldn't have predicted this." Though no one noticed, a scarcely perceptible glimmer of whitish light appeared to radiate from the whiskey bottle, which was in Leon's hand still.

"I get it. I'm wrong again." Amanda pushed her chair away from the table. She tossed her cloth napkin next to her plate of half-eaten dinner and brusquely walked away toward the restrooms. The light from the bottle burst into white luminous spots.

"Amanda, wait," Leon called out. He set the bottle onto the table. Other patrons around the dining room began to stir. Diners stood up, some placing calls and others scrolling their phones in search of weather updates. The low, unsettling peal of thundersnow resounded, vibrating the silverware and eliciting gasps from around the dark room. The glimmer of light in the whiskey bottle intensified into a soft glow.

"Maybe I should go check on her," said Iris, placing her own cloth napkin on the table. Iris had desperately wanted them all to get along, but she was starting to lose hope. In the shadowy restroom, Iris found Amanda with each hand astride a sink basin that looked like it was from the turn of the twentieth century. She was staring into the mirror, where her face seemed to have arisen out of one of those old sepia postcards that Iris had envisioned earlier.

"I just want to say," Iris began, "for the record, that I'm sorry if I ever did anything to offend you." In the dim light cast by the emergency fixtures, Iris could see the hot tears streaming down Amanda's contorted face.

Pushing past her, Amanda said through clenched jaws, "Excuse me. Sister-in-law." Her words reverberated forever afterward in Iris' mind, for that was the last time they ever spoke to each other. Iris and Roman paid the table's bill a little while after the power returned to the restaurant. The tragic events of that tempestuous night were already stamped in time.

Wisconsin Northwoods: 1988

The old Northwoods path twisted and turned for several miles off the main road before coming upon the clearing. The oversized, unwieldy paper map in Rob's hands indicated the trail with a thin squiggly line. The dirt road, hardly wide enough to allow a car to squeeze through between towering pines, came stealing back into Darien's memory. "Yep, this is it," he said.

Darien had not been back to his family's rustic cabin since he was a teen. His hands on the steering wheel were sweaty with excitement at the prospect of finally spending some time together with Rob.

They had been driving all day from Chicago, with the knowledge that Darien's father would be absent from the lake cabin this weekend. Rob asked about him one more time as the car rolled up the gravel driveway, just to be sure.

"He says he's got some out-of-town business to attend to," Darien said. His recently retired father was taking regular road trips to acquire new pieces for his collection, which he kept at the cabin. He had always collected strange and unusual antiques, and now with the extra time, his passion for hunting down personal treasure was exacerbated.

The keys to the front door were in the mailbox. Darien did not remember ever getting any mail at the cabin, which was so remotely entrenched in the forest that the nearest neighbors were rarely seen or heard. The low-lying sun cast lazy shadows of pine trees across the tall grass, imbuing the area with disquiet. The isolated lake behind the cabin was a smooth mirror whose reflection showed the sky of the impending evening. The piney scent of the woods was intoxicating.

"What do you say we build a fire? Should be a lovely night," suggested Darien. The amber light of a late August dusk flooded the cabin from the west. Rob put their bags down in the guest room, not quite knowing how the sleeping arrangements would work. Deep down, he hoped that the single bed in that small room would be a mutual sanctuary for the both of them.

The flames crackled in the stone pit under a clear, starry sky. The two men sat back in their lawn chairs after dinner. They had shared a satisfying meal on the tiny back deck that overlooked the placid body of water. It had no official name due to its isolation, so the family just called it The Lake. The greens of summer had yet to give way to the dramatic colors of autumn.

After careful deliberation, Rob decided to broach a sensitive topic between them.

"Have you given any thought to what we talked about?" he asked.

Darien shifted in his seat. "Not really," he replied.

"Might be something to consider," said Rob, trailing off slightly before adding, "I mean, I would be willing to go through with it." He chose his words carefully, not wanting to ruin this perfect night with Darien.

"That's because you don't know my father," Darien said. "As a matter of fact, chances are pretty good that I wouldn't have a father any longer if it came to that."

It was Rob's turn to be aggravated. He took a deep breath to calm himself. To him, Darien's words were not in accordance with his actions.

"If it came to that?" said Rob. He chuckled nervously. "You're making it seem like a last resort. We can't avoid it forever."

"I wonder if there's anything to drink around here," said Darien. "Should've thought to bring some booze." He sprang from his chair and disappeared into the cabin before the uncomfortable conversation could advance any further. Rob would not be content with their relationship as it stood, and Darien couldn't understand that. Didn't Rob realize would it could possibly do to their careers? Each worked in the burgeoning new field of computers, and men like them were not exactly accepted into any occupational fraternity with enthusiasm. Not to mention the uncertainty with which their families would probably react.

Darien did not find any alcohol in the mostly bare cabinets. He was about to walk back outside to confront Rob empty-handed when the back of his neck prickled. He turned in the darkness toward his father's door, which opened into the largest room in the cabin. Serving as both bedroom and study, his father had it all to himself ever since his parents had separated many years earlier.

The only shape he could make out clearly was the round doorknob, which was engraved with odd symbols. Darien guessed that his father bought it at one of his oddity markets, from which he often came home with peculiar objects and books. He took the cool iron knob in his fingers, turned it, and opened the heavy wooden door.

Through the thin window shades, the light of the half-moon gleamed dimly among the shelves of haphazardly arranged items. Darien still felt that tingling sensation at the base of his skull, almost as though something were regarding him closely.

And then he saw it— a green wisp of light coming from a side table. Inching closer he perceived the contour of a bottle around the light, and the luminous fluid inside. There was no label on the bottle, and a short length of twine around its neck ending in a laminated index card with typewritten text. Darien picked it up, enchanted by the wavering light, which he could swear was growing brighter by the second. Grasping the object, he could tell it was a liquor bottle. Just what he went inside to look for.

A shout came from outside. “Darien, get out here!”

Darien rushed to the door with bottle in hand, half-expecting to see a wild animal in the yard. “What is it?”

“Look,” said Rob, pointing northward above the dense woods. Glimmering forms of pale green light were spread across the firmament like flames from beyond the earth. Above the forest canopy along the lake arose the spectral aurora, a scintillating display backdropped by the vast universe of galaxies and stars.

"Unbelievable," whispered Darien. With their attention arrested by the Northern Lights, neither noticed the whiskey in the bottle begin to swirl, the ghostly green glow now infusing the entire glass vessel. The aurora was extraordinary, jutting its ghostly fingers from the north as if reaching from Lake Superior.

"Don't you see?" Rob asked. "It's a sign." The whiskey was a miniature maelstrom, its green light now approaching the radiance of a lantern as the aurora magnificently lit up the night sky.

"No, I don't see," replied Darien, annoyed at Rob for once again attempting to attribute special meaning to an arbitrary occurrence, to connect it to their own lives. Darien sensed his blood boil, and could not stop himself from continuing. "Look, why don't you give it a rest? It's not going to happen. Not now, not ever." The words left his mouth with far more vitriol than Darien wished. The green-tinged whiskey in the bottle simmered. "You. Ruin. Everything."

Those were the last words spoken on the trip. In the morning Rob woke up early from his made-up bed on the front room sofa, the drumming of rain on the cabin roof. He found a pen in his bag and wrote a note on a napkin: "Walked to the bus stop in town. Enjoy the cabin."

When Darien discovered the note, he knew that he had thrown away the only person who loved him for who he was. The fear in his heart had won out over his feelings for Rob. Gazing out the window at the steady rain, he imagined Rob trudging through mud on the long trail into town. For an instant he thought of running to the car and tracking him down, but a dreadful force obstructed him from within.

It rained and rained, and when Darien's father drove up the gravel driveway in his van a few days later, he was surprised to see his son's car parked there.

Shortly thereafter he found the unopened whiskey bottle lying on the soggy ground beside the fire pit, and wondered how one of the recently acquired objects in his collection of curiosities came to be outdoors. He had purchased it earlier that year at an auction in Chicago, where he learned that the bottle was recovered from a shipwreck at the bottom of Lake Huron.

A little while later, he found his song hanging from the low branch of a pine tree not so deep into the woods. He had used a heavy set of rusty chains dulled with age. And although the rain had ceased the night before, Darien's lifeless body was still dripping wet.

Lake Huron: 1913

"Blood and thunder, you're old." Cal turned from the rail to see his good friend, and fellow deckhand, approaching.

Cal took his morning cigarette from his lips. "Is that right?" He issued a puff of white smoke and a short, dry laugh. The blood orange sunrise cast a dark silhouette around him.

Warren shook his hand, his other pressing against his abdomen. His sailor's jacket bulged in an unnatural way. He appeared to be harboring something as the steamship gently lifted and fell with the swells.

"Forgot it was my birthday until the wind hit my face. It's easy to forget what day it is out here. You lose your sense out on the lake. You know she don't recognize time." He narrowed his eyes at Warren's subtle, wry smile and nodded toward his midsection. "What do you got there?"

"Shh. Take a look." Warren quickly glanced around. There was a small group nearby, but he couldn't wait to reveal his concealed gift. He faced Cal, leaned in, and unzipped his jacket to reveal the top of a bottle of good whiskey.

"The hell you get that? I thought you ran out of the stuff."

"I did, see—"

Cal cut him off. "Don't tell me this is from our stores. You're liable to get locked up belowdecks for that."

Out of the corner of his eye, Cal saw the man they called Jace glancing over. Cal set his jaw and did not look away. As Jace quietly turned back to his own two companions, Cal thought he noticed a flash of amusement on his face. The two men had never gotten along. Not that there was much animosity between them out in the open, exactly, but the younger Jace bore more than a passing envy at how the more experienced sailor was respectfully regarded by all aboard.

Warren couldn't help but notice. "Don't worry about him," he said. Cal tossed his cigarette overboard and took the bottle, sliding it into the wide inside pocket of his coat. For an instant, the crimson light of the morning gleamed off the glass neck.

"What's his problem, anyway?" asked Cal.

"Aw, he somehow got it into his head that you're his competition." Warren said, scowling. "He wants the first mate job, but he knows you're the better man. You've got more years on him, and you know everything there is to know about hauling and steaming. Some people need to tear others down to get ahead." He paused to look at Cal directly. "How about some whisky tonight?"

"Come by for a cup after supper. Thank you, my friend." A chilly gust of wind blew in from the north. "The whiskey'll keep us warm for what looks like a cold front coming in." Warren tightened his scarf as he looked west toward distant, gray skies. Cal went down to his bunk to hide his secret gift on the morning of his fiftieth birthday. His shadow was thrown long across the deck as the darkening horizon in the east announced the passing of yet another day on the lake.

The waves had become tumultuous during supper. By the end of the meal, more than a few bowls of onion stew had crashed to the floor. Cups of suds spilled across the worn wooden tables. The crew hastened to meet the oncoming storm, moving about to lash items to the deck and other necessary preparations. Since the crew comprised seasoned lake men, panic had not yet set in.

Their steamer, the SS *Regina,* was carrying a general goods store worth of supplies. All manner of household provisions was being conveyed northward across the great waters. All they could do now was hunker down in their bunks and hope that the captain and pilot could navigate the tempest. The spirit of the lake would soon prove to be the mistress of their fate.

Warren, tin cup in hand, located his friend among the bustling crewmen. Cal regarded him with a hint of lament in his eyes. "We may have to wait for whiskey until tomorrow. Seas are getting mighty rough." Just as he spoke, a fierce jolt sent them both into the side wall of the cabin. Cries of alarm went up throughout the steamer.

"There he is, bosun," announced a strained voice. Jace had suddenly appeared, pointing rigidly at Cal's head, with the scowling Bosun Anderson in tow.

"What's this about a stolen bottle, Whitmore?" the bosun asked Cal. They all were forced to steady themselves on the rolling ship by gripping the low rafters.

Cal was momentarily caught off guard. "Goddamn you, Jace. Spreading rumors is a dangerous thing for a man to do with no proof." But the bosun was already moving to tear apart Cal's tiny cabin nook.

"Hey, hey, now wait just a minute, you cowardly son of a bitch," exclaimed Warren, who, as he stepped toward Jace, was abruptly thrown forward by the turbulence. The profound boom of thunder reverberated throughout the vessel. The heavy beat down of rain came as the lake was transformed into a maelstrom, whipping the ship around like a toy.

Cal saw Warren's rough hands enclose around Jace's neck, just before the lamp exploded onto the floor and extinguished the flame. The men shouted and grappled as the ship angrily rose and fell on the surface of the cruel waters. The bosun roared commands that were lost within the cacophony of violence. A rush of water cascaded down the stairs that led up to the deck as lightning flickered down the open hatchway. A voice shouted from above, "She's foundering!"

The gale howled in the darkness of the cataclysmic night. None of the crew had experienced as rough a storm. The hull creaked and bent.

"You're coming with me." The bosun gripped Cal by the upper arm, the fighting men now separated by the urgency of the danger. In his free hand the bosun held the bottle of whiskey, which seemed to glow eerily with a dark purple shade of light. He had found it among Cal's things in all the commotion.

Warren was incredulous. "You can't be serious. We're going down here!"

"She'll hold," the bosun responded.

“Wait,” said Warren “It wasn’t him. That’s on me,” he continued, gesturing toward the bottle. A vicious impact hit the side of the ship. A splintering sound resonated belowdecks due to the immense pressure of the waves. The body of the vessel was beginning to break apart. Purple light emanated intensely from the bottle.

“I said that was me, bosun!” Warren yelled as the others left the cramped area, leaving him alone with his escalating guilt.

In a matter of minutes Cal was shackled to an iron bar by a set of heavy rusted chains, where he was told he’d spend the night before being brought to judgement before the captain in the morning. But he never was judged, for the SS *Regina* capsized and sank within the hour. All hands were lost.

The inland sea had swallowed her victims. The stolen bottle of whiskey had been meant as a gift from one friend to another, but ended up lost in strife. The bottle sank to the bottom of the lake, where it would remain for seventy-five years. Lying among the shipwreck, it would ferment with discord in murky obscurity, an agent of emotive potency amid the cold depths of devastating indifference.

Where the Straight Road Was Lost

Steam rose from the surface of the Chicago River like the breath of a submerged beast. The yellow glow of the downtown lights illuminated the windows of the compact car as it drove through the icy, black street in the dead of winter.

"You sure we're going the right way?" asked Zac. It was more a statement of exasperation than a literal question. Much of the filthy slush on the side of the road had congealed into an impenetrable mass, forcing their car to maneuver slowly over banks of weeks-old snow.

"You know, I could have asked a friend to come with me instead. I gave you a way out, but you didn't take it." Cassie fixed her husband with a glare. "Now you're stuck, and you're going to enjoy yourself."

Night arrived early this time of year, bestowing its cold dominion over all. Zac turned the heat down in the car, which had become stifling to him in his overcoat. He unbuttoned it halfway as a relief. The wintry film over the windshield made it difficult to see the lane lines as they sluggishly zigged and zagged around blocks of towering skyscrapers and parking garages.

"Where is this thing taking us?" inquired Zac, zooming into the map on his mounted phone with his right hand, keeping his left on the steering wheel.

Stopped at a red traffic light on a particularly potholed street nearing their destination, the couple was shocked to see a coyote cross directly in front of them. With tawny, mangy fur and a famished look, the coyote deliberately slowed to a stop as it trotted in front of the vehicle. Its focused, yellow eyes were an intensified mimicry of the hazy glow around them. For a brief instant, the coyote seemed to regard Cassie, then turned its gaze to Zac. Within seconds it continued on its way.

The blaring of a horn behind them startled the two out of their shared daze. The traffic light now green, Zac turned the wheel to the left and followed another slim thoroughfare abutted by walls of concrete, the substructures of massive buildings lined with steel gates.

Cassie peered through the car window, trying to follow the animal, but lost track of it almost immediately. “Have you ever seen anything like that downtown?”

Zac shook his head. “No, but I’ve heard there’s been sightings in recent years.” He leaned in to take a closer look at his mounted phone. “Wait. This garage is on a lower level street. The map is taking us under the ground.” No snow plow had traversed this particular road. This being one of the oldest sections of the city, it was too narrow for any truck to enter.

“You didn’t realize?” Cassie asked.

“I just booked a spot with an address close to the condo building. You know, road conditions aren’t exactly ideal to be driving around down there.” Might as well park there now, since it’s already paid for, he thought to himself. “I still don’t understand why you want to hang out with these people.”

“It’s not hanging out. It’s my new boss’s house warming,” said Cassie. The car bounced along the uneven street surface as it approached the dark, cavernous entrance to the lower levels of the city. Its obscurity was exacerbated by the tall lamplights flanking the opening on either side. Thin ice crackled under the turning tires.

"Exactly. Do you hear yourself? These people are your co-workers, not your actual friends. You're just another brick in the wall to them, a cog in the machine." As an adjunct literature professor and amateur guitarist, Zac was fond of quoting classic rock songs as well as books. He went on, saying, "Wendy doesn't appreciate you and all the hours you put in for her."

"Maybe not," responded Cassie, "but I've got to show face. They'll think I don't want to be part of the team." She had been at her new marketing position for a few months now, and Zac had already determined the gist of the company's productivity philosophy: Work, sleep, repeat.

"Abandon all hope, ye who enter here." Zac squinted ahead, the car's headlights tilting downward as it rolled beneath street level. Thick iron columns ahead were posted on either side of the tenebrous passageway. Zac shuddered in his seat. When he glanced at his wife, however, he noticed that she exhibited a curious countenance of expectancy.

"Great," Zac said. "There's no signal down here." The streaming music on the car speakers sputtered to a stop, plunging them into an eerie silence. "We're going to have to read the numbers on the walls."

That would soon prove difficult. Though the car was now safe from snow mounds, decades of grime caked each angular crevice of the sublevel. Monstrous dumpsters were pushed into shadowy nooks. Heavy chains hung from dilapidated fences, their jagged edges disappearing beyond the reach of the gloomy lighting. Here and there, corroded cars were parked alongside the stone walls whose painted signs had faded long ago.

Turning a sharp corner, the rear tire hit an unseen curb and disturbed a flock of pigeons. They flapped their wings in alarm, taking to the air in the constrained space. Cassie noticed how their silhouettes lent them a sinister presence as they fluttered in all directions, as if to escape a vaguely detected threat, residing somewhere down below, that had been awakened by the couple's presence.

Zac stopped at a low-ceilinged intersection and looked both ways while he kept his foot on the brake. A low concrete median separated the lanes ahead, which turned to one lane and curved to the right and out of sight. "I think we go this way," suggested Cassie, pointing to the right.

They hadn't come across any other moving vehicles, which they attributed to the subzero temperature and icy navigation. People did not leave their homes unless they had to. The car advanced, passing loading docks posed menacingly behind folding barrier arms. "Look for a sign reading Beaubien Court," said Zac.

The street they were on seemed to go on for far too long, without a place to turn or reverse. Pus, it grew darker the more they drove, as if the tangible weight of the world were crushing them from above.

"I don't like this," said Cassie, "let's go back up and find another spot to park." At long last, an opening appeared to the right along their single lane. It was a dank tunnel barely wide enough for their car.

"We'll do a three-point turn." Zac moved the car forward a short way into the tunnel, and as he did they saw a hint of light up ahead. "Look," he said, "that's got to be an exit. We can't go back the way we came. It's a one-way, and we can't get across the that barrier."

With increasing anxiety, Zac pressed the gas pedal. The car burrowed deeper into the bowels of the city. It certainly felt like they were driving further downward. They did not see a door or any sign of an edifice for several minutes in this direction. Finally, they came before yet another choice. It was a crossroads with a single lamp hanging from a concrete ceiling that was now only a few feet above the roof of their car.

"Left or right?" asked Zac. Cassie, at a loss for words in this progressing bad dream, merely tapped on the window glass with a ring on her right hand. Click, click. It was a random guess, of course. She had the sinking feeling that they were rats lost in a maze. She had driven Lower Wacker Drive many times, but before today had never sensed a malignancy in the massive subterranean system, as if the city hungered to swallow them whole.

As the car went into motion once again, the vague odor of copper and algae wafted up to the car from an even lower level. They continued to descend down, down, down, curving one way and then the other in the constricting darkness. The barricades on each side of them closed in, their velocity diminishing to a rolling crawl.

"No, no, no," Cassie protested. She looked to Zac, her face a mask of consternation. Perspiration clung to Zac's temples. The next moment, the car found itself at the edge of an unexpected clearing. Looking downward out of the driver's side window, Zac was struck with vertigo to see that they were actually atop a narrow overpass. No floor was under them—only the reaches of open space.

An immense, labyrinthine latticework of crisscrossing bridges and coiling driveways stood before them. There were streets above and below suspended tenuously throughout the otherwise vacuous space, each leading to imperceptible terminals in the obscure distance. There were no other cars on this fiendishly absurd, convoluted structure. The high ceiling was penetrated here and there by twisted steel rods among the cracks. The unbearable stench of aquatic offal offended their nostrils like a fish morgue.

"Where in the hell are we?" Zac's grip on the steering wheel was a vise. It would be impossible to reverse through such a tight passage, so the only option was to go forward into the confusion of interconnected paths. He carefully let go of the brake, allowing gravity to propel the car gently down the slope. On either side of the car, a steep chasm yawned like a cliffside's beckoning void.

The car had steadily advanced by small degrees when Cassie and Zac registered a sound, a subharmonic rumble issuing from the unknown depths.

"You hear that?" Cassie asked. She was too afraid to look over the edge of the thin, swaying overpass. By this point, Zac had completely lost all sense of direction. He noticed one particular ramp leading into an opening in the stone wall just tall and wide enough a for a person but not a car. He intuitively surmised, however, that the tunnel must be leading east, in the direction of Lake

Michigan. Before he could express his deduction to Cassie, she opened the door and stepped out of the car.

"Cassie, what are you doing?" Zac asked. She did not respond.

"Cassie," he said again, but she closed the car door behind her without acknowledging him. A yellow glow coming from the hole in the wall seemed to be intensifying by small degrees. In the light, his wife's face appeared to be mesmerized. Her eyes were wide, her lips slightly apart and manifesting a reflective sheen. For an instant he though he noticed her lips moving, which were too low a whisper to be heard over the car engine. She took a small step forward.

"Cassilda!" Zac shouted, stepping out of the car. He could hear the hushed roar of what must be a mighty body of water. *This tunnel has got to lead to the lake,* he thought to himself. *But aren't we underneath it, then?*

Into the hole she strode. Zac went after her, but her swiftness was phenomenal, otherworldly even, moving like a floating balloon carried away by the breeze down the tunnel. He lost sight of her as he hastened after. The stone ground was slippery with slime, and when he intermittently placed his fingertips on the walls for balance, he felt the sponginess of moist moss. The yellow light from below gained luminosity, coloring the inner tunnel a sickly hue, as if it were the hardened, diseased artery of some colossal creature.

After a minute Zac arrived at the end of the tunnel, which met at the foot of black, lapping waters. The tunnel opened onto a vast clearing, with the stunning dome of the night sky above. Two orbs resembling moons cast a yellowish, overarching haze in the sky, which was punctuated by velvety black stars. Their constellations were completely alien to Zac. Gargantuan towers sprouting from a complexity of intricate architecture sat in the dim distance beyond a dark, glassy lake. The silhouettes of the towering structures gave him the strange impression that they were actually behind the moons.

Presently, he discerned a lilting melody above the hush of the waves. It emanated from a figure not far off in front of him, a woman knee-deep in the water. It was Cassie, of course, softly singing words that Zac could not quite make out. He called out for her again, and when she turned, her face was barely recognizable to him. Her features, so loaded with agitation in the car, had taken on a faraway, inhumanly calm look. She raised her arms in attempt to encompass the mysterious universe around her. Her lips, glistening in the yellow moonlight, parted to mouth her song, now audible to Zac:

Strange is the night where black stars rise,
And strange moons circle through the skies
But stranger still is

–Lost Carcosa.

Cassie sang her darkly sweet verse, and then waded farther out into the water. Zac splashed his way to her, but with each passing moment she seemed unreachable to him, an actor on stage whose role was simultaneously fantastic and real. This place, under the machinery and totality of the city, was both imaginary and actual. Zac saw a woman he knew and loved, but also an entity that linked the present with a place outside of time, a quality he sensed but could never resolve with articulation. She was now part of a dreamscape beneath a city that challenged the limits of stress, and for a second the idea that Cassie had led herself here crossed his mind.

As unlikely as it sounded, she was now equal parts metaphysical vision and materiality. She was finally at home beneath the skies where black stars rise, where twin suns sink behind the lake, under strange moons where the shadows lengthen.

The Missing Captain's Story

Alone, alone, all, all alone,
Alone on a wide, wide sea!
And never a saint took pity on
My soul in agony.

–*The Ancient Mariner*

The drive up to Port Washington was an uneventful. The three of us had decided to depart Chicago early and make the two-hour drive north this Saturday morning for our co-worker's wedding. Today exemplifies the dismal, damp trademark of April in Wisconsin.

Guillermo and Anna chose the first weekend of spring break to get married so they wouldn't miss any class days with our students. That's the kind of couple they are. As for me, Eric, and Johno, we were here to get drunk and have a blast to start our vacation.

The freezing drizzle lets up a bit by mid-afternoon, which is a relief for the wedding party. The diffuse light filtering through the overcast skies, in addition, will lend the outdoor pictures a magical quality. The kind that pauses time and summons an ethereal atmosphere to be captured on film forever. Anna's family, who lives in the area, are already gathering on the roofed veranda of the country club fieldhouse. I follow a wooden staircase that leads down to a muddy garden, where plants and flowers would soon blossom. Beyond the garden is a stone-paved path leading to a cliff overlooking Lake Michigan. The stones give way to a natural trail at which the trim lawn sprouts tall, wild grass matted down by the rain.

Near the cliff's edge grows a dense, woody area. Along the path, an opening appears, like an arched doorway sentineled by pines. The tops of thee trees bend toward each other, creating a canopy of mostly bare branches, their buds yet small protuberances. A strong pine scent mixes with the petrichor and algae lifting from the lake. An old, wooden bench is situated beneath. I take out some tissue I have crammed in my back pocket and wipe some of the moisture off the seat and backrest. I sit down on an acceptably dry spot and gaze out over the lake. The gray, choppy waves oscillate anxiously, as if the waters protested the nuptial proceedings with its turbulence.

Behind me at a short distance, I could make out the chatter of voices from the field house, where the ceremony would take place in a short while. The buzz of human speech is punctuated by random laughter, all of it together morphing into white noise. Simultaneously, the surface of the lake seems to pull at me with its vast, mesmerizing chaos. I am frozen to the spot—transfixed, as if gripped and held by the elements. I wonder at the expanse of the inland sea under darkened skies, the horizon a gentle kiss between the two half spheres.

Off to my left I hear heavy footsteps treading on the soggy undergrowth. Their plodding sound is a spell; an odd sensation that my solitary space has been intruded upon. The din of the wedding crowd sounds muted as though cotton is jammed into my ears. If I were to look back, I would expect to see nothing but open, untamed land without a trace of civilization.

Dark brown shoes stop a few feet away. Mud is caked around their outer soles. The bottom hems of a coarse pair of deep blue pants are soaked. It is an older yet sturdy man with a thick, salt-and-pepper mustache amid a five o'clock shadow. The bags under his eyes suggest a life of sleeplessness and stress. He's wearing a black pea coat and cap, looking overly rugged for wedding attire. His clothing gives off the same algaeic odor as the lake.

"Wedding guest," he says. His rough voice startles me.

I glare at him suspiciously. Apparently, he takes that as an opening.

"Out of Erie town did we set forth eastward on an April morning before dawn. Thunder broke forthwith, with the waters black as the seas of Hell. An old steamer it was, but true, and we called her the SS *Vivienne.*"

"Excuse me, sir," I say. "Are you here for the wedding?" I jerk my head in the direction of the field house behind us. Not waiting for a reply, I ask, "How do you know Guillermo and Anna?"

"I captained the crew of twenty-four worthy men into the heart of Lake Erie. That day we saw neither star nor heard whisper, save the wake of our precious *Vivienne.* I tell you, only the devil knows the darkness of its icy soul. The devil and me."

"I'm sorry, are you the captain of a ship?" I ask. "So, you don't know the newlyweds?" Who is this guy? I begin to feel uncomfortable.

He tugs on his mustache before proceeding. "Before the living light appeared behind the clouds on the next day, I was awakened by my chief mate, pounding rather roughly on my cabin door."

I squint over my shoulder to see some of the other guests going back into the field house. The ceremony must be starting momentarily. I glance at my watch to confirm, but also to send a message that I'd have to be getting back. The man doesn't take the hint, however. It's irksome that someone would assume my audience like this. He even has the gall to sit next to me on the bench.

"'Cap,' he shouts from the other side, 'there's something you gotta see.' With a crew of seasoned men, I says to myself, this better be important. So, I grab my coat and don my cap as the mate leads me astern, where there's a group of them peering over the rail like a murder of crows."

"Okay, I'm sorry," I start to say, "I need to—." But then something unusual takes place. It's like a tremendous weight suddenly burdens my shoulders, an invisible burlap sack of sand. I realize I can't stand up. I'm able to turn my head, though, and when I do, the captain and I make eye contact. It might just be the powers of fancy in my mind, brought on by the transfixing effect of the lake, but his brown eyes glimmered in the afternoon shadow.

They mesmerize me. I am nailed to the spot. Behind me, the buzz of chatter has died out.

"'Look there!' cries a deckhand, pointing into the waves." The old captain leans his ruddy face close to mine, and lowers his voice to a soft growl. "Can you believe what we saw? A serpent, thick as an ancient tree trunk, over two rods long. Aye, 'bout the length of our steamer it was. The color of smoke, with black pupils smooth as billiard balls. It slid through the water tireless and easy, following in our wake. Was then I knew the journey was cursed."

I hear resounding piano music carry from the ceremony. It's the percussive gait of the Bridal Chorus. I'm missing the start of the wedding. And yet, beyond explanation, the captain's words glue me to the seat with preternatural force. Further, the thrust of his anecdote, as unlikely as it is, begins to swell with the gravity of a parable. There's a truth I intuit but would not be able to articulate.

"Through all the day, the serpent faltered not in its pursuit. My crewmen fulfilled their duties as they should, yet the devil swims swift. Before the second cloak of night fell, I summoned all on deck. Since taking leave of Pennsylvania, the crew had been ill at ease, and now we knew why. We'd prayed for the stars to show, but to no avail. So, I decided to confront Erie's terrible worm, an infection in the watery muscle of her lean torso. The crew followed me to the rail at the stern. In my room I kept an old harpoon I acquired in New Brunswick a number of years prior. There's no need for it on the Lakes, but I held on to it like a totem all the same. Yet only then had it revealed to me its fated purpose."

"Please," I start, but I am literally spellbound. The old captain's eyes are two lasers compelling my attention. What makes it worse is being absent from the wedding. I also wonder what my friends, Eric and Johno, must be thinking among the congregation. The harder I strive to formulate a thought, however, the more difficult it is to concentrate on anything other than the captain's beguiling tale. I am an insect caught in his web of words. And so I give in.

"I hove the harpoon to my shoulder, like so," the captain goes on, demonstrating as he speaks. "And for an instant we saw eye to devil eye. He raised his monstrous head above the waves. In the black glimmer of its silvery scales, I thrust with all my might. The point of my harpoon penetrated between its obsidian eyes. He thrashed and died. The crew hoisted it so that the pale face of the lifeless creature lay on deck, and his extensive body hung into the water. I took my knife, lifted his heavy lip, and slashed his gums. The dark blood flowed. And I lifted *this* unto the anonymous sky."

The captain sticks a hand under the collar of his shirt and extracts a cream-colored object about the size and length of his middle finger. It was a pointy tooth, tied to twine like a pendant. My jaw dropped in mute disbelief.

"The crew of the ship cheered like madmen. I saved the doomed voyage by killing the devil creature, they claimed." The captain put the tooth away, back underneath his shirt.

Bells peal behind us, signaling the end of the wedding ceremony. The pre-dinner cocktails and hors d'oeuvres are now being enjoyed, no doubt. Despite the cool weather, beads of perspiration roll down my forehead. I wipe away the sweat with my sleeve.

I remember once watching a nature documentary about predatory birds. The narrator claimed that when the prey was captured, it enters a mental state of disassociation, where the reality of their fate is momentarily appeased before their demise. That's how I feel.

"'Fore we knew it, we'd steamed our way steady to the mouth of the Detroit River. Ever since I hanged the devil's tooth round my neck, the elements were on our side. The crew was in good spirits, but the sentiment would prove to be short-lived. Lake St. Clair was a looking glass, a hoary-green reflection of the gloomy skies. A change had charged the air. We felt the shift in our bones. As we traveled further northward, an arctic wind rushed to meet us.

"Like a fetus out the womb of Lake St. Clair, our *Vivienne* entered the river on the north end of the lake under ever-darkening skies. It was nighttime in the day, and cold as the deepest pit of Hell. The River St. Clair labored to urge our steamer forward through her freezing canal. The ice was thin, but think was the sense of impending disaster among the men. We crushed through the frozen face of Huron and were birthed unto a dark, icy sea."

I shiver in my seat on the old, wooden bench. It isn't just my imagination—it's getting much chillier here near the cliff's edge. The sounds of clinking glass and silverware drift over from the wedding celebration. Dinner is served. I'm sure Eric and Johno are hungrily wolfing theirs down. And here I am, paralyzed in some strange, nautical theater. Anger bubbled up from my gut. That, and the reedy tendrils of fear.

The captain strokes his mustache and continues.

"Through my telescope I spied the craggy chunks of floating ice as far ahead as I could see. It was a nightmare to look upon. We'd must needs abort our delivery of lumber to Port Washington, it seemed. The crew, as if mimicking the weather, turned cold against me. My chief mate was hearing whispers. Cap, they said, has cursed the voyage. What formerly seemed a vanquishing of the devil was clearly revealed to be a deception, they said. It is the vile tooth, they said, that hangs about Cap's neck, what troubles the ship.

"We dropped anchor. In my cabin, I took note in my logbook of the decision to turn back. Huron was too formidable in her late winter stubbornness. But then a mighty curious thing happened.

"Against my bare chest, the devil tooth stirred. At first it was scarcely perceptible. I clutched it, but it quivered still, even lifting itself like a feather in the breeze. At the same time, my brain's deep fibers stirred. Holding the infernal tooth in my fist, I opened my cabin door and took the two stairs down onto the deck. All the crew were below. The icy, black world was frozen in time. Finally, the clouds parted to reveal an immense bowl of stars. When I reached the bow, immediately I heard the first thundering crack."

The captain grips me like a statue with his glittering eye. Pausing for dramatic effect, he takes out the tooth once again and holds it aloft. In the short distance, where with my peripheral vision I perceive the soft glow of the party lights, music pulses. The guests must be dancing, drunk in their revelry.

"No—it was not the sound of a lightning bolt. It was the ice commencing to break apart! The bergs split as if amid the blasts of the trumpets of Jericho themselves. They moaned, screeched, and sang their beautiful, hideous song. I heard more than saw in the darkness of night—a cacophony of fractured voices calling out from the heart of time itself. The devil tooth shuddered in my palm. At once, the crewmen stumbled up the stairway and onto the deck to apprehend the puzzling sounds emanating from the surface of Huron.

"Some fell to their knees beholding a miracle. Some howled in bewilderment. Others gazed daggers at me as if I were the devil himself. What should have been a cause of relief—and my own triumph—dissolved into huddled confusion.

"The collapse of the ice went on for hours, a symphony of cracks and explosions. The crew was rapt with awe. Just before dawn, I gave the command for anchor aweigh. We maneuvered up the eerily calm lake while ice masses parted like the Red Sea. The journey was smooth as glass. We saw no sign of fish nor fowl all the day long. The men avoided making eye contact with me. My chief mate, too, seemed to see in them a novel power."

Ironically, I hear the clinking of a handful of ice dropped into a glass. The unlikely echo triggers another thought, one that I can't believe I hadn't thought of. My cell phone. I could use it to message Eric or Johno. Wait, no. It's in my jacket pocket, unfortunately, which is at the moment on a coat check room hanger. The stench of seaweed on the old Captain's breath dominates the air. He must chew it like tobacco, I fathom.

The old captain draws closer. I feel the waves of coldness emanating from his body. The hair on my arms stand on end.

I sense his narration about to reach an unpredictable climax.

"As the *Vivienne* passed through the Straits of Mackinac, I became terribly weary. It only then dawned on me that I hadn't slept a wink in over a day. Pinned haplessly to the bow of our steamer, I had altogether lost track of time. Some form of otherworldly energy possessed me. So, I called to my chief mate and bade him take the helm, to instruct the steersman in the navigation of upper Lake Michigan. We had passed through the ice. The devil tooth was tranquil.

"I stumbled to my cabin with swollen feet and heavy eyelids. I told my chief mate to wake me after we crossed mid-lake, which would be several hours away. The weather, though still biting cold, was endurable. Before closing my door, I observed that the lake resembled a boundless painting created by the hand of a silent god. I dropped onto my bunk and slept a dead sleep."

I hear the joyful clamoring of voices. Some guests stepping out for a refreshing breath of crisp air, no doubt, or to perhaps smoke a cigarette and toast to the future with a glass in hand. But I cannot call out, or speak, or move. The captain's incantation has got me in its inescapable grasp.

"Some time later I awoke with the healing scent of the lakes in my nostrils," the captain goes on. "Late afternoon light invaded my cabin through the porthole. My chief mate had not woken me, so I figured our pace was slow. Without thinking, I sought the devil tooth round my neck. It was still there, of course.

"However, it is what happened the minute I opened my cabin door that continues to plague my mind.

"The first thing I noticed was the lack of human sound. No footsteps about the deck or talking among the crew. I heard only the lapping of the cold waves against the hull. I peered from stern to bow and so no one. They were all belowdecks, you might guess, which would be in dereliction of their nautical duties. You would be wrong.

"I took the stairs down from the hatch. Not only was my crew of twenty-four men gone, but the steamer showed no sign of them ever having been there. I pounded my head with my palm, trying to shake the echoes of a bad dream. The world had taken on a peculiar, oily sheen, as if I myself had entered that boundless painting. I wondered how I should be able to bring the *Vivienne* home all alone. That's when the winds came howling, and the waters became agitated."

As he spoke these words, a piercing gust strikes. Scattered, fat raindrops accompany a low rumble of thunder that originates from somewhere behind us, reverberating across the dark lake. It does not phase the captain in the slightest.

"Angry waves broke over the railing and onto the deck. The ship rocked from side to side, lifting on the huge crests and smashing down into each trough. It was as sudden a gale as I've ever seen rip through these lakes. Under my shirt, the devil tooth—that of the Erie serpent—trembled. The horrific sound of the fracturing hull shook me to my core. It was broken like bread in the hands of a mad god.

"I was living an impossibility. My crew was gone! Were they all dead? To where had they disappeared? Was I afflicted with insanity? Amidst these questions, the whole cursed business would come to an end with my bones lying on the floor of Michigan herself. But then, from somewhere west, between the steamer and the land, a dark shape materialized. At first, I figured it was a fata morgana, but no-- it was a real ship headed in my direction.

The tempest swirled with vigor. My beloved *Vivienne* was foundering. With a lifesaver round me, I hit the cold, cold waters. It robbed the very breath from my soul—and, in truth, I have never recovered.

"The next thing I remember is being laid out and shivering on a bunk aboard the SS *Rebeque.* One of their deckhands spotted me in the fearful weather and lowered a boat. How they did it, I shall never know. The storm, they said, abated the moment they dragged my limp body onto the deck. The captain wanted to know about the rest of my crew, for he saw I also wore a captain's garb, but I was dumbfounded. They would not have believed me anyhow, and would have sent me straight to the asylum. In the end they probably figured I'd suffered enough. Perhaps the icy water had numbed my brains.

"The *Rebeque* delivered me to the beach of Port Washington ere nightfall. Indeed, the very one just below this cliff. Immediately the steamer turned back round and the left the shore. She disappeared into the enveloping dark."

Car engines zoom out of the parking lot. Lightheaded, I finally stand and stretch my limbs, at first unaware of how warped and distorted my time on the bench actually had been, as if the night were a malleable bar of black gold hammered into an impossible shape. The story seems to have abruptly ended. My senses and emotions return. Bafflement, however, quickly replaces my displeasure at having missed the wedding, for the captain himself is gone.

"Where the hell have you been?" Johno asks.

Needing a drink, I signal to the bartender. "Didn't feel good," I lie. "Went to the hotel to lay down." I scan the walls and ceiling of the establishment, which are covered with nautical-themed decorations and artifacts.

Eric was incredulous. "You serious?" He takes a swig from his beer bottle. "You missed the whole night, man. You better now or what?"

"Probably food poisoning," I say. "From those burgers we stopped to eat on the way up here." I point at the bottle in Johno's hand and tell him, "Order me one of those." Doing my best to avoid this conversation, I quickly step away toward the bathroom, where I splash my face with cool water.

On the way out of the bathroom, a picture on the wall of the corridor catches my attention. It is a black and white photograph portrait of a mustached man. My arms prickle with goosebumps. Underneath his picture is a formal, cursive name: Captain Ambrose H. Clarens, 1932. Below his name it reads: SS *Vivienne.*

I'm suddenly dizzy. The music in the bar becomes surreal static, my pulse hastening to sprint-level speed. I stop a woman wearing a polo shirt with the name of the bar stitched on it. She looks busy, but I've got to ask.

"Excuse me," I say, gesturing at the photo, "do you know who this is?"

"Oh, that's the missing captain," she says.

"The who?"

"We call him 'The Missing Captain.' You must be from out of town. Anyway, in the 1930s, they say he went to take a nap on his ship one afternoon on the lake. But when the guys in the crew went to his cabin to wake him up, he was gone. No sign of the captain—he just completely disappeared. Never to be found again."

"Oh? That's strange," I say. "I've never heard of that."

"Yeah," the woman says, "if you grow up in this town you just kind of learn that story. Not only that. It's said he still walks up and down the shore to this day each April, telling his side of the story. He's supposedly been seen on the beaches and cliffs around the area, like a lonely ghost." I feel the blood drain from my face.

She's about to stride away when I ask one more question. "What do you think happened to him?"

She shrugs. "Have no idea if that story is even true, but maritime folks in the area have always sworn that it is. Like most stories about the lake, I guess, there's a mixture of truth and myth."

I nod in thanks and go back to the bar, where my friends are talking and laughing loudly. Johno hands me my bottle of beer.

"Still don't believe it," Eric says, shaking his head at me. "Why do you smell like seaweed?"

I take a swig from the bottle and look at him. "It's just your imagination," I say.

Afterward: Crossing Death's Door

Unlike the rest of the fictional stories in this book, the following personal narrative is nonfiction. Thank you for reading.

On a warm day in July 2023, I boarded a ferry from the northern tip of Door County to Washington Island. Door County is a finger of land that juts out from the east side of Wisconsin, with the island situated just beyond its reach. The gap between the end of the land and the island is the strait called Death's Door. The ferry traverses the four-and-a-half-mile gap of Death's Door several times per day, carrying cars and the families who own them.

With me on that mild summer day was my own family, including my wife and two daughters, my parents, and sister-in-law. We had all loaded up our vehicle for an excursion northward from my Chicago home, with a week-long exploration of Lake Michigan shores in our sights. I have held a lifetime interest in Great Lakes maritime lore ever since my father used to drive our family to the city's coast of Lake Michigan when my brothers and I were kids. I recall the wonder of looking out across the lake, which to me seemed and endless sea. What lay beyond the horizon of the inland seas captured my imagination, and fomented a feeling which has never left me. Since that time, my father and I shared a love for the history of our home region, from the ancient glaciers to the establishment of the Chicago portage.

Many of my road trips since those times have included stops at history museums, shipwreck sites, and natural land formations along the lakes. Having never visited Washington Island, I decided it would be apt to go on my birthday. I was intrigued by the tantalizing concept of traveling across the door of death on the day of my birth.

The legend of this nautical passage goes back hundreds of years. Also known throughout the centuries as Porte des Morts, this name graces some maps even to this day. The French epithet was most likely coined in the seventeenth century. In the days of sailing ships, the danger of the passage was due to shoals that are tricky to navigate, as well as the rocky shores of its isles.

Written reports of several early frontiersman tell of a battle between indigenous groups at Deaths Door, during which up to one hundred Native Americans drowned. The most likely scenario offered by historians of the region is of a conflict between the Potawatomi and Winnebago tribes. During the battle on the strait, according to reports, a storm claimed numerous lives on both sides. This event is one of the first recorded instances of the infamous Great Lakes gales, which are known to strike without warning. One account describes a monstrous, rogue wave that pulled a band of men off a rocky island ledge.

As I gazed across the blue-green waters on my birthday, I wondered how many skeletons still lay at the bottom of Death's Door, covered in soft algae. We were passing over the graves of warriors, explorers, and laborers. Meaningful lives that were lost to the forces of the Great Lakes elements.

The volatile channel may have also played a role in the disappearance of the *Griffon,* the largest vessel on the Great Lakes at the time. This legendary ship was built by explorer Rene-Robert Cavelier de La Salle, the seventeenth century French explorer. It was by all accounts a magnificent marvel of maritime architecture, inspiring awe in the indigenous peoples and fur traders alike.

Carrying profitable cargo, the ship traveled throughout the waterways of the Eastern continent, from Niagara Falls, down the Mississippi River, and across the Great Lakes.

The final place the ship had likely anchored was Washington Island. On a windy September day in 1679, the *Griffon* set sail carrying thousands of dollars' worth of fur merchandise. The ship never made its delivery, however. In fact, it was never seen or heard from again. It was the disappearance a mythical vessel, whose current whereabouts is the supreme mystery of Great Lakes seafaring lore. Although no conclusive evidence exists to prove the exact point of the ship's foundering, the role of Death's Door in its story cannot be discounted.

A saga of shipwrecks continued with regularity after La Salle lost his beloved *Griffon.* The Wisconsin Historical Society has rigorously collected details of what they deem the hazards of Death's Door. From 1837-1914, no less than 24 wrecks occurred on the turbulent waters of Porte des Morts, with a multitude more in the surrounding area before and after this time period. One shipwreck that particularly resonates with me is the wreck of the *Forest,* which departed Chicago in 1891with a load of cargo to the northern reaches of Lake Michigan. On my July 2023 trip, I also had departed my Chicago home for the north end of the lake, in search of a deeper knowledge of Great Lakes history. And, perhaps, an elusive spiritual connection that was sown during my childhood visits to its shores.

In his book *The Moribund Portal,* Richard Gavin writes about places where significant loss of life has occurred. He explores the idea that sites of tragedy are imbued with an eerie character, a spectral resonance often strengthened by the passage of time. This ghostly presence, writes Gavin, may be the trace of an immaterial channel, a portal through which the living have passed to the land of the dead. No site represents this concept more fittingly than Death's Door, whose history of archaic shipwrecks pervade the geography with numinous soul. This is where the spirits of the drowned still live.

On the late afternoon ferry trip back to contiguous land, the sunlight out of the west struck the lake's surface with a golden-amber hue. My two daughters stood with me at the upper rail, the exhilarating wind in their hair. The hum of the motor coupled with the sound of the splashing wake combined for a hypnotic effect that capped off a memorable day on the beautiful beaches and fields of Washington Island. Much of its wilderness remains mostly unchanged from the days of the French explorers who crossed this untamed territory in centuries past.

From the upper deck of the ferry, I looked down to see my father, who at that moment was enjoying the closeness of the water. Its spray glided lightly in his direction, dispersing like a prism as the waterdrops caught the sunlight. Here he was at Death's Door, the place I had brought him to experience, on the lake to which he had introduced me. He faced the bow, looking homeward.

That was the last boat trip my father would take. He passed away suddenly less than a month later. Recently, as I perused family photographs and videos, I came across a home movie recorded by my father on a 1980s camera. The video shows me as young boy, no older than four or five, playing on the concrete steps at the edge of Lake Michigan. The video was taken on a cool, breezy, overcast day. I have a fall jacket on, and we seem to be alone at this inlet near the Adler Planetarium. Whitecaps dot the grainy surface of the lake. You can hear my father's voice, calling out to me to be careful near the water's edge. But I was invigorated. My fate had been sealed. I would incessantly strive to understand the lake in all its triumph and tragedy.

Various worldwide myths tell of nautical passages which souls must cross from waking life to the afterlife. There is the Mediterranean Sea in Greek mythology as a metaphor for the liminal space between life and death, as well as the River Styx of the underworld. In Buddhist mythology, the recently deceased are challenged to traverse the River Sanzu, and in Norse mythology the Gjöll waterway separates the lands of the living and the dead. These are merely a few examples.

The night before my father's passing, I stood by his side as he slept. As his eyelids moved as if dreaming, I envisioned him on a boat, advancing toward a celestial horizon. I imagined him crossing Death's Door, the lake's light spray on his face like a baptism, the sides of his favorite flannel shirt fluttering like wings on the wind.

Acknowledgements

Each story in this book was inspired by the legends, myths, and historical events that make up the treasury of Great Lakes tradition. In my research, I've found that much of the untold lore of the lakes is expansive, far more so than what is represented in this limited collection. Although my home library features a healthy section of books on this topic, I've also spent much vacation time traveling to the museums, libraries, and spots of interest along the lakes.

For these experiences, I thank my family for accompanying me on my trips, and often patiently waiting for me, while I perused every point of interest in detail. Each shipwreck, artwork, exhibit, artifact, pamphlet, statue, fossil, historical plaque, and book shop.

I want to express appreciation for the editors who have believed in my work and published stories that appear in this book, especially Rob Carroll of *Dark Matter Magazine* and C.F. Page of Strange Elf Press.

Immense thanks to author Pedro Iniguez, who kindly read an advance copy of this book and provided a wonderful quote for the cover.

Thanks so much to Dr. Jesu Estrada of Harold Washington College for their support, and for providing me with opportunities to publicly talk about my writing. Thanks also goes to Robert Bitunjac of the Chicago Public Library for his support and invitation to talk about my books.

Thank you to Christopher Hawkins and Shawnna Deresch of the Chicagoland chapter of the Horror Writers Association for their continual support!

Thank you to all my readers.

About the Author

Aleco Julius is the author of *Endless Depths: Cosmic Themes, Weird Lore, & Hidden Knowledge*. His writing appears in *Vastarien, Hellebore, Cold Signal Magazine, Myth & Lore, Anterior Skies,* and more. He has contributed to books from Anathema Publishing, including *Seeds of Ares* and *A Wayfarer's Hearth*. He has also written essays for the *Holland Files.*

Look for his stories in *Dark Matter Magazine,* and the anthologies *Negative Creep, Always Night,* and *Writer's Retreat: Tales of Writing & Madness.*

Find him on Instagram: @dagger_of_the_mind

He lives in Chicago.